WILD, WILD WEST

Rising from behind and vaulting across the hood of the nearest car, the big Texan continued to move with surprising speed. The Mob enforcer let out a profanity and sent his right hand under the left side of his jacket. The movement was duplicated at an even greater speed by the blond giant. Twisting the big British-made Webley-Fosbery .455 automatic revolver from the spring-retention shoulder holster, he brought it clear, and slammed the six-inch-long hexagonal barrel against the mobster's cheek.

"Call a paddy wagon and have him hauled off to the pokey," the blond giant said, having handcuffed the unconscious man. . . .

Books by J. T. Edson

THE NIGHTHAWK
NO FINGER ON THE TRIGGER
THE BAD BUNCH
SLIP GUN
TROUBLED RANGE
THE FASTEST GUN IN TEXAS
THE HIDE AND TALLOW MEN
THE JUSTICE OF COMPANY Z
McGRAW'S INHERITANCE
RAPIDO CLINT
COMANCHE
A MATTER OF HONOR
RENEGADE
WACO RIDES IN
BLOODY BORDER
ALVIN FOG, TEXAS RANGER
HELL IN THE PALO DURO
OLE DEVIL AT SAN JACINTO
GO BACK TO HELL
OLE DEVIL AND THE MULE TRAIN
VIRIDIAN'S TRAIL
OLE DEVIL AND THE CAPLOCKS
TO ARMS! TO ARMS, IN DIXIE!
TEXAS FURY
THE SOUTH WILL RISE AGAIN
BUFFALO ARE COMING

Mark Counter's Kin

J. T. EDSON

A DELL BOOK

Published by
Dell Publishing
a division of
Bantam Doubleday Dell Publishing Group, Inc.
1540 Broadway
New York, New York 10036

ISBN: 0-440-21047-X

Printed in the United States of America

Published simultaneously in Canada

December 1994

10 9 8 7 6 5 4 3 2 1

RAD

*For Samantha and Trevor, with
my sincerest thanks for making
me a grandfather twice and introducing
me to Masters Darren and Dean Page.*

AUTHOR'S NOTE

When supplying us with the information from which we produce our books, one of the strictest rules imposed upon us by the present-day members of what we call the "Hardin, Fog and Blaze" clan and the "Counter" family is that we *never* under any circumstances disclose their true identities, nor their present locations. Therefore, we are instructed to *always* employ sufficient inconsistencies to ensure neither can happen.

We would like to point out that the names of people who appear in this volume are those supplied by our informants in Texas and any resemblance with those of other persons, living or dead, is purely coincidental.

We realize that, in our present "permissive" society, we could use the actual profanities employed by various people in the narrative. However, we do not concede a spurious desire to create "realism" is any excuse to do so.

As we refuse to pander to the current "trendy" usage of the metric system, except when referring to the caliber of certain firearms traditionally measured in millimeters—i.e., Walther P-38, 9mm—we will continue to employ miles, yards, feet, inches, stones, pounds, and ounces, when quoting distances or weights.

Contents

PART ONE
JAMES ALLENVALE *"BUNDUKI"* GUNN
In
A GOOD TIME WAS HAD BY ALL
1

PART TWO
DEPUTY SHERIFF BRADFORD "BRAD" COUNTER
In
A SMUGGLER—OR IS HE?
15

PART THREE
SERGEANT RANSE SMITH, COMPANY "Z," TEXAS RANGER
In
PERSONA NON GRATA
59

PART FOUR
JESSICA AND TRUDEAU FRONT DE BOEUF
In
THE PENALTY OF FALSE ARREST
91

PART ONE

JAMES ALLENVALE
"BUNDUKI" GUNN

In

A GOOD TIME WAS HAD BY ALL

Although Ambagazali could not compete with Kenya in size, it was considered to be beaten only by that country in the volume of tourists who came to help support its healthy economy, and the number of attractions offered for their entertainment. Certainly nobody who visited the capital city of Ambaga could deny the Black Rhino Hotel was equal to the best anywhere else in Africa and its Big Five Room rated high among the most luxurious restaurants in the continent. The cuisine was excellent, whether "local" dishes or the finest type of banqueting from Europe and the United States. Therefore, despite the high prices charged and the fact that there was only a single sitting for dinner each night, business was invariably good and the chances of obtaining a table without having a reservation were practically nil.

As usual, on that particular evening, the Big Five Room was full. What was more, in addition to the normal variety of clientele, a group of *very* important people were present in a party hosted by Prince Simba Nyeuse, the well-liked and respected ruler of Ambagazali. King Latu Kham and Queen Mei Kwei-Ho of Camchakton in Southeast Asia were his guests of honor. Others at the table included Cyrus D. Hollinger, a film producer from Hollywood whose stated intention was to "bring back 'message'-free action-escapism adventure movies to the cinema, along with the audiences who used to pay to see them." He was accompanied by the stars of the movie *Lorna, Ruler of the Jungle,* which he had just completed shooting on location in the country, Donna Lindstrom, Marla Thorton—respectively the beautiful heroine and equally glamorous villainess—and the handsome, muscular hero, David Blackett. Also at the table were Colonel Sandru Katamundoni, head of Ambagazali's Bureau of Internal affairs, and the King's Chief of State Security, Colonel Lom Tak.

Toward the end of the meal, before the thick locally made carpet could be removed from the open area in the center of the room to allow dancing to commence, attention was drawn away from the VIPs' table and its illustrious occupants.

"What a *magnificent* couple," a female diner gasped, her accent that of a Texan and her attire suggestive of great wealth.

A similar sentiment was being uttered at several tables around the room.

Nor could anybody suggest the description was inaccurate.

The man and woman who entered had looks and physiques unequaled even by the trio of film stars.

Six feet three in height and in his early twenties, the man had shortish wavy golden blond hair and almost classically handsome tanned features. Like the majority of customers, he was dressed formally. The white tuxedo he wore set off a physical development that would not have been judged out of place if he had entered for a "Mr. Universe" competition. The great spread of his shoulders trimmed to a narrow waist set upon long and powerful legs. However, for all his great size, he showed no sign of being slow or clumsy in his movements. Rather, he carried himself with an easy grace that was indicative of a potential for speed when required as well as Herculean strength.

About the same age and measuring five feet eight, the woman seemed an ideal mate for her companion. Curly and cut short, her tawny hair framed exceptionally beautiful features whose lines denoted breeding, strength of will, and intelligence beyond the norm. To add to the suggestion of wild, almost primitive, freedom that she exuded, clearly powerful, yet not unfeminine, muscles played under smooth skin just as bronzed by the elements as that of her companion. Unadorned by jewelry of any kind, but enhanced by the rich golden tan, the plain halter-necked and sleeveless white satin evening dress she wore established that she possessed the kind of figure many a "sex symbol" movie actress sought to attain. The contour-hugging fit of the garment, its skirt slit high enough along each side to give tantalizing glimpses of her shapely legs in black stockings and high-heeled red mules, proved beyond any doubt that her most curvaceous form was not produced by any kind of artificial aids.

"Who are they?" asked the husband of the woman from Texas, whose fortune was derived from the oil business in that state. "The feller puts me in mind of Big Andy Counter, or his cousin from Amarillo, Ranse Smith."

"He's more like young Bradford Counter, the one who's gone to being a deputy sheriff down to Rockabye County," the woman declared. "They're 'like enough to be *twins*."

"His name's James Allenvale Gunn," replied the local businessman who was guest of the Texans. "They call him 'Bunduki'—!"

"Bunduki?" the woman interrupted. "But that's the Swahili word for a gun, isn't i— Oh sure, now I *get* it. His surname's 'Gunn'—!"

"You've got it all right, momma," the Texan admitted dryly, although his attention was not directed at the young man under discussion.

"Who is he, Joe?" the woman asked, eyeing the blond giant with open admiration.

"He's the adopted son of Lord Greystoke—" the businessman began.

"You mean Tarz—?" the woman asked.

"Since all those movies supposedly about him were made, especially the most recent, he prefers that people call him Lord Greystoke," the businessman interrupted. As he went on with his explanation he nodded from the young man to the VIPs' table. "Anyway, Bunduki's the Chief Warden of the Ambagazali National Wildlife Reserve and a good friend of the Prince."

"How about the girl?" inquired the husband, and received a coldly disapproving glare from his wife.

"She's his cousin, Dawn Drummond-Clayton," the businessman supplied. "Runs the Physical Culture Class at the Ambaga University and is training our team for the next Olympic Games."

While the conversation was taking place, the couple were crossing the floor toward the VIPs' table. However, before they arrived, two big and bulky men with the currently fashionable "designer" stubble on their faces rose and, leaving behind a young blond woman almost matching Dawn in looks, height, and form, they slouched forward until confronting the handsome young couple.

"All right, man," said the taller and heavier of the pair, his deep voice having the somewhat guttural accent of those who would have been called "white settlers" in earlier decades. "What's the idea of not giving Willie and me the shooting licenses we asked for?"

"Yes, man," the second man supported. The words came out as "Yis, men," and his tone was indicative of similar origins. Jerking his thumb toward the beautiful and shapely young woman at their table, he went on, "Minna, Carl and me want to knock down a couple of bloody leopards that's been living off our *watu's* goats."

"The last time it was elephants that were damaging the maise *shambas*," Bunduki replied, knowing the Swahili word *watu* was being used in this case to mean the workers on a farm rather than people in general. "And before that, you said a pride of lions were taking your cattle. This time, I want *proof* before I turn you loose to start shooting."

All the locals in the room and some of the visitors understood what the conversation was about!

To preserve the wildlife of the country, but also to avoid friction with farmers and others who suffered from depredations by animals, Prince Simba Nyeuse, with the help of Bunduki, had established rules that were both fair and generally effective. Except in clearly defined areas and under *very* strict supervision, no hunting of any kind was permitted throughout Ambagazali. However, it was accepted from the beginning that the rights of the human population must be protected. Therefore, in addition to the Game Department taking punitive action where necessary, a farmer was allowed to shoot any animal that was killing his stock or endangering his workers.

To prevent abuses of the ruling, those creatures that provided the most valuable salable commodities—the skins of leopards and lions, elephants' tusks, and the horns of rhinoceros, for example—were designated "royal game." While a permit to shoot would be issued, providing there was proof of guilt, the entire carcass of the animal was classified as property of the State. That did not mean it was wasted. Rather, it was used to help fund the Game Department and alleviate whatever financial loss had been incurred by the complainant. After it was valued for sale, the price of the damage it had inflicted was given to the injured party and the Department received the remainder. Naturally, human nature being what it is, although there was not as much money to be made as would come from a private sale, there had always been, and would always be, those who tried to circumvent the ruling for their own profit.

"Are you calling us *liars,* man?" Carl challenged, looking menacing.

"Have it any way you like," the blond giant answered calmly. "But come to my office in the morning and we'll talk about it there."

With that, Bunduki stepped forward and, surprisingly in view of their threatening demeanor, the pair moved apart as if to let him pass. However, as he was doing so, Willie caught him by the shoulder and jerked him around to send a blow to his jaw that drove him into Carl's open and waiting arms. Encircled by them, he was held by the shorter man so the larger could step forward and drive another punch, this time into his stomach.

Startled exclamations arose from all around the room. However, even as the maître d'hotel was about to signal for the burly members of the staff who served as bouncers on the rare occasions such duties were required, his attention was attracted by a gesture from Prince Simba Nyeuse. Reading the meaning of the prohibitive wave that was given correctly and noticing Colonel Katamundoni was restraining the Oriental officer at his side, the maître d' concluded there was no need for preventive measures to be taken. Although puzzled by his ruler's attitude, he waved back the men who had started to move toward the open space and awaited developments with interest. What was more, following the example of the royal party, the other customers remained in their seats and watched what was happening.

Before Willie could continue the attack, Dawn Drummond-Clayton set about rendering assistance to her cousin. Emerging from the slit in the skirt, her right leg delivered a powerful kick to his assailant's rump. Letting out a profane exclamation, the burly man turned and, placing the palm of his right hand against her face, he gave a shove that sent her reeling until brought to a halt by reaching the table he and Carl had vacated. Judging by appearances, she was neither incapacitated nor frightened by what had happened. Giving a hiss of anger, she started to push herself forward. However, rising and overturning her chair, Minna intervened. The grab she made hooked her fingers into the low-cut back of Dawn's gown and, as she gave a pull, there was a ripping sound as the material burst open.

Granted a momentary respite by his cousin's intervention, Bunduki made the most of it. As Willie turned his way, he braced himself against Carl and swung his feet from the floor. The thrust he delivered with them to the barrel-like chest sent the larger of the men away as effectively as the tawny-haired girl was removed. Bringing down his feet, he stamped the left upon the toes of his second assailant, which elicited a yelp of pain and caused the grip upon his arms to be relaxed. Throwing his own apart with a surging heave that displayed his magnificent muscular development to its best advantage, he escaped from the hold and pivoted to crash home a right cross that slammed its recipient backward a couple of steps.

Realizing what had happened, but apparently oblivious of her far from oversized black lace bra, briefs, and scarlet suspender belt being brought into view, Dawn forgot about going back to aid her cousin. Instead, she spun around and lashed a slap that rocked Minna's head sideways. Then, plunging her fingers into the extreme décolleté of a black satin evening dress as revealing as her own, she repaid the damage by giving a wrench that split it asunder down the front. Instead of showing embarrassment over having her no more substantial bloodred undergarments displayed, the blonde retaliated with just as hard a backhand blow. Although the impact rocked Dawn on her heels, a moment later their fingers were buried into one another's hair and, losing their mules—which were ill adapted for such strenuous activity—they went in a twisting stagger toward the center of the open space.

Retaining his footing and lowering his head, Willie rushed forward like a bull buffalo launching a charge. Proving that the suggestion of agility he exuded was correct, Bunduki stepped aside at the last moment. As he blundered by, Willie received another kick to his butt. This time, it proved more efficacious and he was propelled onward until reaching the wall. However, Carl had been allowed a respite and swung the blond giant around to send a punch into his chest that drove him backward. Following up the attack, the smaller of the pair was less successful with the kick he launched. Catching the rising ankle in both hands, Bunduki subjected it to a twisting heave that caused Carl to flip over and alight with a thud on the floor.

Changing tactics when clear of the tables, Dawn released Minna's hair and caught her by the right arm to pivot and subject her to a shoulder throw with speed and precision. Breaking her fall with an indication of skill as she came down, the blonde brought up her feet. Bending over with the intention of continuing the attack, Dawn had them rammed against her body and she was pitched forward in a somersault to descend supine on the thick carpet. However, she too arrived in a fashion that proved she was just as competent at avoiding the worst effects of such treatment. Instead of tackling the tawny-haired girl immediately, Minna rolled across the floor to grab Bunduki by the right leg and sink her teeth into his calf. Her attempt to hang on to the limb for long enough to let her companions capitalize upon the distraction was ended by Dawn diving after her. Grabbed by the back hair, she was compelled to release her hold and was hauled away until able to twist around and catch her assailant by the flapping skirt of the badly torn white dress.

Although the relief produced by his cousin was welcome, Bunduki was far from being out of danger. Rebounding from the wall as if he were a rubber ball, Willie was returning swiftly to the fray. What was more, proving that he had escaped the worst effects of the throw, Carl was starting to get up. The blond giant's white jacket had burst along the back seam under the strain caused by his struggles and he shrugged himself clear of it before the larger attacker reached him. Ducking beneath a looping right swing that was hurled his way, he slammed his fist into Willie's midriff. However, he was prevented from following up the blow by seeing Carl plunging toward him.

Feeling the garment being torn even more, Dawn inadvertently completed its destruction by releasing the hair she was grasping and jerking backward to leave its remnants in the blonde's clutching hands. Then she hurled herself onto Minna and they began a rolling, hair-pulling, wildly struggling mill that took them across the floor.

The furious and apparently mindless tussling they were engaged upon caused holes to burst in their stockings and saw the blonde lose her dress.

For a few more minutes, the clientele of the Big Five Room watched a fight that they would long remember. What was more, accepting that the occupants of the VIP table had no objection to its taking place, they began to show their appreciation verbally by rooting for the tawny-haired girl and the blond giant. However, despite the display of support, nobody offered to rise and lend them physical assistance after a man who made an attempt was ordered to refrain by the nearest bouncer.

Set upon by one or both of the big men, Bunduki defended himself with a skill in using his fists, feet, wrestling skill, and ability at general roughhouse brawling against the best they could do. Nor was the fracas between the girls any less vigorous. In addition to the primitive feminine tussling, they proved they too could employ more effective tactics. On occasion, each proved she possessed considerable skill as a boxer and a wrestler. At one point, sent between them by a kick from Bunduki, Carl was set upon by Dawn and the blonde with a fury that saw his shirt ripped off to expose his hairy and much-tattooed chest before he could escape.

However, although none of the spectators attached any significance to the matter, there was no blood drawn from any of the combatants despite all that was being done. Nor, except for the loss of a ruined stocking apiece when they parted company with the straps of the suspender belts, did the furiously struggling distaff side of the brawl tear away any more of their skimpy remaining garments.

Finally, having knocked Willie through the front entrance, Bunduki sent Carl after him with a kick to the ribs. As he did so Dawn and Minna, staggering and swaying uncertainly, launched punches that arrived on the other's jaw simultaneously, and both went in a twirling dive to the floor. Having disposed of his second attacker, the blond giant crossed to where the girls were facedown and trying to force themselves exhaustedly into a kneeling position. He picked up one under each arm and carried them, hanging limply across his crooked elbows and as if they were no weight at all, after the men.

"Ladies and gentlemen," Prince Simba Nyeuse called in excellent and accent-free English, causing silence to descend on the room. Tall, slender, and with the copper-red skin pigmentation that emphasized he was of the Nilotic Ambaga nation, he was good looking and wore the smartly cut khaki uniform of a Field Marshal in his Army. "I hope you weren't alarmed by what has just happened. It was merely a demonstration of the kind of action you will see when *Lorna, Ruler of the Jungle* appears on the cinema screens." Gesturing to where, smiling and showing no animosity toward one another, the perspiring and heavily breathing "fighters" returned through the door, he went on, "Please allow me to introduce you to the stunt team for the production, Minna Brownlow, Willie Dayton, and Carl Strothers. They were assisted by my good friends, Dawn Drummond-Clayton and Bunduki Gunn." Waiting until the laughter and applause that greeted the announcement died away, he continued, "The performance was in aid of the Gazaliville School for the Blind and I trust you will all show your appreciation for it by donating generously. By the way, you were probably too engrossed in what was going on to notice, but we have had video cameras filming it, and when the tapes have been edited, copies will be on sale for the same good cause."

"That was a most remarkable show you put on, Bunduki," King Latu Kham praised, his English as good as that of his host. Of medium height and in his early thirties, he was handsome in an Oriental fashion and had on black evening clothes of Occidental cut. "And you too, of course, Dawn."

"I have a feeling Latu found your part of the fight the more interesting, Dawn," small, petite, and beautiful Queen Mei Kwei-Ho remarked with a smile.

"I hope none of you are going to ask for a live action replay," Dawn Drummond-Clayton replied. "Minna might enjoy doing that sort of thing, but I prefer wrestling with pythons."

Half an hour had elapsed since the end of the staged fight that had been organized by Simba Nyeuse for the entertainment of his guests. All the "combatants" had taken a shower and were now dressed in a fashion suitable for them to be presented to their royal audience. While they were cleaning up and changing their clothes, Cyrus B. Hollinger had explained that, in addition to working as technical advisers for the location and animals sequences, Dawn and Bunduki had volunteered their services when the other stunt team who were working on the movie contracted dysentery and could not participate in the climatic "fight" between the heroine, the hero, and the "baddies." He also told how the performance that evening had come about.

On hearing that his friends had proved most adept at picking up the fighting routines, Simba Nyeuse had requested a demonstration and, ever willing to obtain what he felt sure would serve as excellent publicity for his movie, the producer had suggested how this could be done to the best advantage. Wanting to help the film people, for whom they had formed a liking—also because they considered they would be giving support to a worthy cause—Dawn and Bunduki had agreed to play their part. Already having been taught how to "pull" kicks and blows, or react when in receipt of similarly faked attacks, they had spent the past two days practicing the dialogue that provided the reason for the trouble and the moves that had made the "brawl" appear so genuine.

The outer clothing that was ripped off the "combatants" of both sexes had been of a "tear-away" variety specially designed for such a purpose. However, despite the "fight" in the movie having ended with them both "topless," Dawn had been disinclined to go that far when she knew there would be a number of friends and acquaintances present. To prevent the removal occurring by accident, Minna had produced the skimpy, but specially strengthened, under-garments. As a further precaution against accidental loss, the bras were secured by an adhesive coating that retained them in position regardless of their being well filled and subject to the strenuous activities in which the wearers were engaged.

Because of the response from the other spectators, especially with regard to the size of donations made for the support of the Gazaliville School for the Blind and sales of the video film, the five performers considered the time they had spent rehearsing the "brawl" and the exertions expended producing it had been well worth the effort.

"Be that as it may," the King said. "My own martial arts team couldn't have bettered your show."

"But they always fight genuinely, don't they?" Dawn suggested, having seen the men and women in question perform on television newscasts and heard a statement to that effect.

"They do *not*," the King denied with a grin. "After the money I spend having them trained, I'm not going to risk any of them being killed or seriously injured just to perform for a television camera."

"You're giving away State secrets, dear," the Queen warned in a mock chiding fashion, then turned her gaze to Dawn and Bunduki. "And I'm sure you and your three friends all deserve some kind of award for your performance."

"So do I," the King seconded, but changed the subject as he saw the girl and the blond giant were showing embarrassment. "By the way, Bunduki, Simba has told us how you came by your nickname."

"Did he also tell you how, when I was young, they called me Toto ya Bunduki?" the blond giant inquired.

"No," the King admitted. "What does it mean?"

"Son of a gun," Simba Nyeuse supplied with a grin. "And if telling you *that* doesn't deserve some sort of an award, say being thrown to the crocodiles in the Tangana River, I don't know what does."

PART TWO

DEPUTY SHERIFF BRADFORD "BRAD" COUNTER

In

A SMUGGLER—OR IS HE?

"You know something, Tom," Deputy Sheriff Bradford "Brad" Counter remarked sotto voce, his accent that of a well-educated Texan. "Uncle Ranse was *right*!"

"I've never known him to be," Deputy Sheriff Thomas Cord asserted, just as quietly. The timbre of his voice indicated he too had been born in the Lone Star State, albeit hailing from a lower stratum of society. Several years older than his companion and some six inches shorter, with auburn hair tinged gray at the temples, there were grin quirks at the corners of his mouth that belied the professional hardness of his darkly tanned face. He had a stocky, yet firmly fleshed, build that indicated he kept himself in excellent physical condition. "What'd he manage to get right at last?"

"Stakeouts *are* the worst and most miserable duty any peace officer can draw," Brad replied, showing no offense at the apparently disparaging comment about a kinsman for whom he had the greatest respect as he knew his companion shared the sentiment. "He always told me so and, by cracky, he was *right*."

Such was the exceptional potency of the reproductive genes imparted by their great-grandfather, Mark Counter, anybody seeing the young peace officer and his cousin, James Allenvale "Bunduki" Gunn, together for the first time might have been excused for believing that—despite the latter being a year older—they were twin brothers. The physical resemblance was remarkable, especially when considering it was shared by at least two more of Mark's descendants.

An undercover assignment Brad had recently undertaken for the Rockabye County Sheriff's Office resulted in his having to have his golden blond hair given what an earlier generation called a "crew cut," but he was just as classically handsome and had a "Mr. Universe" type of physique matching that of Bunduki in almost every detail. There was, in fact, less than half an inch difference in their height and other bodily dimensions. What was more, the peace officer was the equal of his cousin in strength and agility. While their ability at bare-handed fighting was about the same, because of different needs in their respective ways of life, Brad had greater skill in the use of firearms—especially handguns—and Bunduki was better with other, more primitive, weapons.

The Rockabye County Sheriff's Office had county-wide jurisdiction and the Gusher City Police Department did not, so much of Brad and Cord's work involved dealing with cases for both organizations that were usually the jurisdictional responsibility of detectives in the Homicide Bureau. Therefore, following the example of their predecessors in the Old West, they generally wore civilian clothing when carrying out their duties. However, the assignment upon which they were engaged that warm and moonlit June evening was not within the confines of

Gusher City, seat of Rockabye County. Because of the need for them to be easily and immediately recognized as peace officers should the information upon which they were acting prove correct, they both were wearing the official uniform for their department.

Both deputies wore the prescribed tan-colored, low-crowned, and wide-brimmed J.B. Stetson hats, but they had removed the well-polished gold and silver five-pointed star badges of office from the front of the crowns. Their khaki military-style shirts had a dark-blue shield with "Sheriff's Office, Rockabye County, Texas" in white letters on each upper sleeve and a similar badge—albeit suitably dulled to prevent its glinting in the moonlight and possibly giving away their position among the bushes in which they were hiding—was pinned to the left breast pocket. Matching slacks, a black necktie, and brown rubber-soled boots completed their clothing. Indicating length of service and his seniority as a deputy sheriff, there were three inverted chevrons on the sleeves of Cord's shirt. Having a flashlight, instead of the long wooden "night stick" occasionally carried in daytime, on a loop at the left side, a key ring, pouches for spare ammunition, and handcuffs were interspersed between it and the holster for their handguns on the right. Their black Sam Browne–style waistbelts did not have the shoulder strap of the original design.

Being aware of how great a part individual choice played in such an essential matter, the policy of the Rockabye County Department of Public Safety allowed all the local peace officers to make their own selection of handguns and the rigs in which these were carried. Having taken a fancy to the Colt Government Model of 1911 automatic pistol, Brad had had the one he owned modified to increase its potential and wore it in a forward-raked Bianchi Cooper-Combat "bikini" holster—so-called because of its small size—with a long-tanged Elden Carl "fly-off" leather safety

strap. Roughly pear-shaped, passing over the fully cocked
hammer of the pistol and attached to the holster only by a
press stud, the strap retained the weapon securely for normal use while permitting a speed of withdrawal that his
illustrious great-grandfather—no slouch in such matters—
would have been hard put to match. Cord's four-inch-bar-
reled Smith & Wesson Model 19 "Combat" .357 Magnum
revolver was in a more conventional-looking holster of the
type made popular by Assistant Chief Patrol Officer William H. "Bill" Jordan of the United States' Border Patrol.

However, because the assignment upon which they were
engaged could entail dealing with armed men who were
willing to fight back, the two peace officers were supple-
menting their basically defensive firearms with more potent weapons. Although there were more modern weapons
available at the Sheriff's Office, because of personal pref-
erence, Cord had chosen a .30-caliber U.S. M1A1 carbine
with a folding skeleton stock and Brad had a Winchester
Model of 1897 "trench gun" across the crook of his left
elbow.

"I've known *some* who liked stakeouts," Cord commented, as if imparting information of the greatest importance. "But then, I've known some who liked beating
themselves with birch twigs, come to that."

"You're sure seen *life,*" Brad declared, eyeing his older
and far more experienced companion in a sardonic fashion
that implied a genuine liking and admiration for one he
knew to be a master of their trade. Then he returned to his
earlier subject. "Hell, I've never known time to drag this
bad."

"Shall I help pass it quicker by telling you some of my
jokes?" Cord suggested.

"Why thank you 'most to death," the blond giant replied, making a face as if he had bitten into a lemon. "But,

with all due *disrespect* to my *elders,* I'd sooner let the time drag."

"That's funny, *boy,*" Cord drawled, sounding as if he believed such a contingency was impossible. "You're not the *first* who's told me the same."

"And I bet I'm not the *last,*" Brad asserted, his partner having acquired a well-deserved notoriety for telling "shaggy dog" stories and other jokes that the other members of the Sheriff's Office claimed were the worst in the world. Then, having glanced at the luminous dial of his wristwatch, he became more serious as he went on, "Do you reckon Willie the Thief's taken me for a sucker, Cord?"

"Not if I know him," the older deputy assessed.

"But why'd he contact *me* and not one of the old hands at the office?" the blond giant queried, worried by the possibility that the first information of its kind he had been able to supply to his superiors and upon which he, his partner, and some of the other deputies from their Watch were acting might prove false.

"He's been away a fair spell and looked to be short of cash when we saw him downtown," Cord answered. "Knowing him from back when, once he learned who you are, he'd figure, you being new to the Office and likely wanting to score points by making arrests, you'd be willing to pay more than the rest of us for what he had to offer."

"I remembered what you told me about dealing with stoolies," Brad declared. "When he let on he'd got something for me, I said that, seeing as it was the first time we'd done business, it would be pay by results."

"And he didn't ask for something on account?"

"Nope. He said that would suit him fine."

"Then he figures what he's told you is true."

Despite nothing having happened so far, and the time

approaching two o'clock in the morning, the blond giant
was rendered less perturbed by his partner's summation.

Developed at the suggestion of his uncle Ranse, one asset to his work of a peace officer that Brad possessed was
the ability to remember faces and, more important, be able
to connect them with the appropriate name. While going
to collect his imported M.G. MGB convertible from the
parking lot of the Upton Heights Shopping Mall where he
had been purchasing some underclothing the previous afternoon, Brad had been stopped by a man he recognized
and who claimed this was mutual. Cord had pointed him
out earlier in the week as being Willard "Willie the Thief"
Cosset, a stool pigeon who had left town about six months
ago. The nickname had originated from his habit when
accused of being an informer of responding in an injured
tone, "A stoolie, me. Hell, everybody knows I'm a thief!"

Introducing himself, after having looked around to make
certain they were not being observed by anybody who
might later remember the meeting to his disadvantage,
Cosset had said he could supply information about a noto-
rious Mexican smuggler—or rather a suspected smuggler,
as guilt of this crime had never been established—who
would be making a delivery of unspecified contraband
across the Rio Grande. Having learned when and where
this was to take place and settled the matter of payment,
Brad had reported what he had been told to his partner
and their Watch Commander. Although they had warned
him that numerous attempts to catch Alonzo "Tricky Al"
Nevada in the act of handling contraband goods had failed,
they had agreed to follow the information up. It would,
First Deputy Angus "Mac" McCall said with a suggestion
of satisfaction in his dry Scottish burr, put the Sheriff's
Office one up on the Border Patrol and local Customs
officers—with whom they would be cooperating—if they

could achieve what their friendly rivals had repeatedly failed to do.

On being told of the information, the heads of the Border Patrol and the United States Customs had said they would not be able to assist in making the arrest. All their men were committed to an operation against a gang of large-scale dealers in narcotics and, as Tricky Al had always refused to handle such a commodity, they considered he rated a lower priority. Being equally aware of the Mexican's record with regards to drugs, Sheriff Jack Tragg and McCall had agreed with the decision. Claiming they could all benefit from some good healthy exercise and night air to "blow away the cobwebs of city living," the First Deputy had also asserted the matter could be handled by his own men without needing assistance from the other Watch or—apart from a courtesy offer to the one responsible for the area in which the operation would take place—any of the Sheriff's Sub-Offices.

Although Brad was relieved to know he would be working with the members of his own Watch, who were already showing signs of accepting him as one of their number because they considered he had proved his worth to their satisfaction, he had not been completely at ease. He was still too recently appointed and conscious of the unconventional means by which this had been achieved to want the onus of mounting the present operation placed upon him. Nevertheless, guided by Cord—who would nominally be in charge as the senior member of their investigative team—he had studied maps and, with the cooperation of the deputies from the local Sub-Office, selected the place at which they would confront Nevada. Cosset had known the night, but was unable to say at what time the crossing of the Rio Grande would take place. Lacking this knowledge, the blond giant had decided to commence the stakeout at ten o'clock.

The party was composed of those members of Brad's Watch selected by McCall, the local deputies, and, as an additional backup in case any of the smugglers should succeed in escaping from the others, two officers from the Gusher City Police Department's Canine Patrol and their attack dogs. They had driven to a rendezvous in the vicinity of their ambush position. Then, leaving their vehicles far enough away to avoid detection, they had gone on foot to the chosen position and concealed themselves among the fairly dense bushes that grew along the bank of the river and flanked the only path between it and the nearest open country.

Despite everybody having acted as they would if a more experienced member of their department were responsible for the operation, Brad had found the waiting irksome. What was more, as time dragged by without there being any sign of the smuggler, he had felt his anxiety growing. Nor had his feelings been soothed any by knowing stool pigeons sometimes sold information of dubious quality to recently appointed peace officers who were eager to "score points" by making arrests and who were willing to hand over their own money to bring this about. The only consolation he had been able to draw was remembering he had acted upon the advice received from his partner in refusing to pay for the information until after it was proved valid.

"Could be he—!" Deputy Sheriff Bradford "Brad" Counter began, still worried in spite of his partner's reassurance.

The sentence was not completed!

Before the blond giant could finish, the most welcome sound he had ever heard came to his ears. Although there might be a number of perfectly harmless and legal reasons for the clatter of approaching hooves and saddle leather creaking on the other side of the river, he took comfort from having been told this was the means most frequently employed by Alonzo "Tricky Al" Nevada when bringing contraband into Texas.

Regardless of the change in Brad's attitude, he was not fully at ease until he saw the party that emerged from the bushes on the Mexican shore begin to come across the river!

In the lead, dressed after the style of a Mexican *vaquero* and riding a horse with easy competence, was a short, stocky man whom the blond giant had no difficulty in identifying as "Tricky Al" Nevada. The suspected smuggler was followed by half a dozen mules, to each of which ran lead ropes for a string of five equally well-loaded packhorses tied tail to halter one behind another. A further five apiece were led by a burly and tough-looking Mexican attired in a similar fashion to Nevada, and a tall, slim young white man. Having shoulder-long hair and a pallid face that was not improved by a drooping "Zapata" mustache, the latter was bareheaded. Clad in a loosely fitting *kaftan,* embellished by "peace beads" and a C.N.D. insignia on its chest, ragged Levi's pants and sandals, he would have appeared more at home with some "liberal" protest march than helping to run contraband into Texas. Looking ill at ease in the saddle, he clearly lacked the riding ability of the other two. Despite the number of animals involved, the trio comprised the whole party and none of them gave any indication of being armed. In the case of Nevada, this came as no surprise. According to all the reports Brad had seen, he never carried weapons.

Crossing the river without difficulty, the water being reasonably shallow at that point, the three men led the pack animals ashore. Studying them as they came over the wide and gently sloping bare bank and then along the narrow trail, Brad was not impressed by what he saw. In comparison with the paint mare ridden by Nevada and the mules, the rest of the horses were a pretty sorry lot. However, it was obvious they were considered adequate for the task of carrying the bulky panniers attached to their saddles. Wondering what these contained, he decided the time had come to close the trap he had set and that now seemed likely to prove fruitful.

"Peace officers here!" Brad shouted. Although he had been told Nevada spoke fluent English, he was employing the challenge—which Sheriff Jack Tragg had selected as being the most suitable way of avoiding confusion when a peace officer's presence was announced under such conditions—in his native tongue, mainly for the benefit of the lanky white man. "Stop and raise your hands above your heads!"

As if in echo to the blond giant's words, they were repeated in Spanish by a Hispanic deputy who could claim truthfully—should the need arise during a trial—this was his "native tongue." Such a precaution was necessary to prevent a defense attorney trying to assert his client had failed to understand an order given in English as he did not have a sufficient command of that language.

While the orders were being given, Brad and the rest of the ambush party advanced swiftly from their places of concealment. However, except for the two shouted commands, they moved silently to avoid frightening and possibly stampeding the horses. Although the movement was intended to cut off any attempt at escape by the trio, none was made. Instead, the burly Mexican and the white man released the first of the horses they were leading and rode forward until they were one on either side of Nevada. Only then did they duplicate the action he had already made by starting to raise their hands.

"No, *hombre*!" Brad snapped, also speaking the Spanish of the Texas and Mexico border country, as the larger of the Mexicans made a gesture as if intending to reach beneath the left side of his *bolero* jacket. "Keep that right hand going *up!*"

"Stop trying to scratch that flea, Tomas!" Nevada ordered over his shoulder, speaking English with an almost theatrically singsong Mexican accent, as the order was accompanied by a warning gesture from the Winchester trench gun in the blond giant's hands. He had already raised his hands and went on, "You have to excuse my cousin Tomas, *Senor el Policia.* He doesn't wash too often and gets fleas which bite him bad."

"What's the meaning of *this?*" demanded the white man, his voice having a high-pitched and whining timbre common to some sections of San Francisco.

"Now that's strange," Deputy Sheriff Tom Cord drawled. "We were just going to ask you the selfsame thing."

"I demand to—!" the white man spat out.

"Now, *Senor* Purser," Nevada put in soothingly. "There's *nothing* to be worried about. The *Senores el Policia* are just doing their duty by stopping us, although I can't think *why* they're doing it."

"We're sort of nosy, Al," Cord explained. "So, seeing you coming over here at this time of the night, we're wondering what you've got on those horses."

"That's none of *your* goddamned business," Phillip Purser claimed, having the typical middle class–middle management "liberal's" hatred of all forms of law enforcement officer unless his own interests were being protected by them. "We're not living in some Right Wing Fasci—!"

"Way all those scum-rades talk," a deputy from the Sheriff's Office commented in an Irish brogue just loud enough to reach the ears of the scowling "liberal," thereby bringing the heated words to an end. "You'd think they didn't have police in any of the Commo countries."

"There's no need to talk that way!" Nevada asserted

coldly and his English momentarily improved as his tone hardened, but his words were clearly directed at his white companion and not the Irish peace officer. Reverting to his previous accent, he continued, "I can see how us coming over this way might look just a little bit *suspicious* to them, so they are only doing their duty by being here and they have the right to ask us our business."

"Why, I'm right pleasured to hear you say *that,* Al," Cord declared in what seemed to be a warmhearted tone, having assumed control of the situation by virtue of his seniority and in accordance with departmental policy. "So how's about you telling us why-for you're coming over here at this hour and what those packhosses are toting."

"Certainly, *senor,*" the suspected smuggler obliged, just as amiably. "It is easier and cooler traveling at night, especially with such poor horses as are all I, being an honest man, can afford."

"I'll buy that, about the horses anyways," Cord drawled sardonically. "I've never seen such a sorry bunch of crowbait, so what're you carrying on 'em?"

"Mexican and *Indio* artifacts such as your *Americano del Norte* tourists like to buy," Nevada replied. "Nothing expensive, or really *old, senor.* I mean, they're not valuable antiques, or some of our national treasures."

"You mean they're *fakes*?" Brad suggested, paving the way in case he should be required to play the hard-nosed one if he and Cord were to employ the "good cop-bad cop" ploy to gain information.

"They are *not!*" Purser denied indignantly, resenting the blond giant for having been so much better favored in looks and physique as much as for his being one of the "Fascist police." "Every one is made by a Mexican or an Indian using the methods employed by their ancestors for centuries."

"They're what I've heard called 'recent antiques,' *senor,*"

Nevada elaborated, with a glare that implied he wished his white associate would leave the talking to him. "Although I think there are some who would call them *junk*. But what do I care. I get paid to fetch them over to Gusher City is all I'm interested in."

"Then you won't mind happen we look them over?" Cord suggested.

"I *do*!" the "liberal" snapped, reaching beneath his *kaftan*. "We've permits to import them!"

"I'm not gainsaying it," Cord drawled and waved his left hand toward the packhorses. "Only I reckon the sheriff and the good old boys of the U.S. Customs'd like to know why you're fetching them over this way."

"That was *my* idea," Purser claimed, overlooking how the suggestion had come from Nevada originally. "I'm a member of the Society for Encouraging the Use of Energy-Conserving Transport. Bringing them this way saves using gas and, in addition to this being a shorter route, leading so many horses along the freeway in the traffic would be too dangerous to contemplate."

"I can see how it would," Cord admitted. Although he had never heard of the organization, he did not doubt it existed. What was more, he could envisage how its purposes could be utilized for Nevada's ends. "But we're still going to have to look over everything in the packs."

Watching the "liberal," Brad could see that he intended to continue the protest. However, at that moment, his mount snorted and began to void itself in no uncertain fashion. Giving it more attention than he had devoted to it earlier, the blond giant could not remember ever having come across such a miserable-looking creature. Roman-nosed, prick-eared, cow-hocked, and sway-backed, it showed signs of being nervous and high strung. To add to its ill-favored appearance, blotched by grayish-white patches, its coat was a washed-out yellow color such as he

had never seen before. Glancing at the pile of dung behind
it and noticing the pungent aroma being given off, an idea
came to him.

"Hell!" Brad said, reaching into his right breast pocket
to produce a whistle, which he twisted between his fingers
in an apparently pensive fashion. "I've forgotten to signal
for the backup boys to come in."

Feeling sure Nevada would have envisaged the possibility of there being other peace officers in the vicinity to cut
off attempts at escape, so he was not giving away any secret
law enforcement procedures, the blond giant raised the
whistle to his lips. On blowing through the mouthpiece,
there was only a slight sibilant hissing sound and not a full-
throated blast.

However, the effect upon the ugly-looking horse was far
in excess of what might have been expected from the sound
being emitted. Letting out a frightened snort, it reared surprisingly high on its hind legs. A howl of alarm burst from
Purser as he was shot backward over the cantle of the
Mexican-style saddle and slid backward to land rump first
in the steaming, evil-smelling mound. Letting the trench
gun slip from his left hand and allowing the whistle to drop
and dangle by the chain securing it to his pocket, Brad
sprang forward to catch the animal by its headstall.

"Blast the whistle!" the blond giant growled, having no
difficulty in bringing the horse under control. "It must've
got plugged up."

Satisfied it was safe to do so, Brad released the animal.
Then he raised the whistle once more. This time, although
he did not employ as much air pressure, his blow elicited a
deeper blast. Nor was he surprised by the result. A present
from his uncle Ranse, the whistle, in addition to looking
and sounding like an ordinary police whistle when so required, changed its function when the mouthpiece was
turned as he had done while taking it from his pocket. He

had turned it again before the second blow so that it no longer produced a tone pitched too high for the human ear to detect but audible to dogs and other animals. To ensure only the "liberal's" horse would take alarm, he had directed the blast straight at its prick ears and his estimation of its reaction had proved correct.

"Search all you wish, *senor*," Nevada offered, having joined in the laughter that greeted the mishap to Purser.

"Why thank you 'most to death," Cord accepted. "Only we'll not do it *here*. There'll be light and we can see to do it better at the Sheriff's Sub-Office in Shipman."

"There wasn't a *thing*," Deputy Tom Cord reported in a disappointed tone. It was shortly before noon on the day after the stakeout, and he and his partner were reporting to their superiors in the Watch Commander's Office. "We looked in every one of the vases and pots they were carrying, but they were all empty. Customs sent along a couple of their boys with a fluoroscope and other gear, but got zilch. Nothing but adobe showed up when the doodads were put in front of the 'scope and they checked out right for weight, so there wasn't any gold or jewels put in when they were being made. All the permits for bringing them into the U.S.A. were in order, and the reason we was given for coming over the river with them on horseback makes sense. Al claims they meant to let Customs know where to find them as soon as he got to a telephone, and that scumrade Purser confirms it."

"So we still don't have anything on good old Tricky Al?" Sheriff Jack Tragg stated rather than inquired.

"Nothing that we could try to make stick in court without some knee-jerk 'liberal' legal eagle claiming we're just being vindictive against his client," Cord agreed. "In my opinion, it'd be wasting *our* time taking them before a judge with what we've got."

"I'll go along with that," First Deputy Angus "Mac" Mc-Call seconded dourly. As always, even though in his office, he was wearing his hat. Rumor claimed that, because he slept with it on, not even his wife had ever seen him without it. However, as a concession to his superior being present, he had surrendered the only chair in the room and was standing behind the desk. He claimed restricting the seating prevented people from dallying unnecessarily and wasting his time. Far from being a source of annoyance in the Sheriff's Office, both habits were regarded by the deputies as the harmless idiosyncrasy of a hard-pressed and competent administrator. "He's slipped through our hands again, blast it."

"I'm sorry, sir—!" Deputy Sheriff Brad Counter began, having tried without any noticeable success to see from the faces of his superiors how they regarded the abortive efforts he had been responsible for setting in motion.

"Like John Wayne says, 'Never apologize, it's a sign of weakness,'" Jack Tragg drawled. "You've just joined a large and exclusive club, Brad. Let me welcome you in behalf of the other members who are present."

"I still don't know how he took *me*," McCall admitted. "How about you, Tom?"

"I wish I could figure out where I went wrong," Cord declared. "And last night wasn't a *total* loss. I do declare the scum-rade smelled *better* after Brad caused the *accident* that dumped him butt first in his horse's droppings."

"I've a letter from him complaining about what happened, Brad," the sheriff remarked, showing amusement rather than disapproval. "It will get a suitably apologetic reply. There's one thing comes to mind, though. Al could have been running a straight consignment through, so's to throw us off guard for when he fetches some real stuff over later."

"Shall I tell Willie to—?" the blond giant began, wondering whether he should pay for the information even though it had failed to produce the required end result.

"Brad!" the sheriff interrupted. "Don't *ever* again mention the real name of a snitch to *anybody* except your partner. And that anybody even includes Mac and me."

"Aye," the first deputy supported. "Always use a nickname you settle between you. He's *your* man, and it's up to *you* to give him all the cover you can."

"I'll remember, sir," Brad promised, annoyed at having forgotten the same rule he had been given by Cord.

"Tell your snitch to keep on the ear," Tragg instructed, feeling sure the mistake would not be repeated.

"There's one thing, though," McCall went on, sharing the sentiment. "Doing it doesn't mean you can miss out on the Range Qualification Shoot tomorrow."

"As if *we'd* do a thing like *that*," Cord said with an air of injured innocence. "There's *nothing* I like better than the Range Qualification Shoot."

"Unless it's filling in reports," McCall suggested and glanced pointedly at the empty wire tray marked "In" on his desk. "Which reminds me—!"

"We're just going to make it out now," Cord asserted, knowing the meeting was at an end.

"When my partner says *we*," Brad went on. "He means *me*."

"R.H.I.P., boy," Cord pointed out, using the abbreviation for "Rank has its privileges." "Let's go and get her done."

"You know something?" Deputy Sheriff Tom Cord remarked. "Even though the steering wheel's on the wrong side and I haven't used a stick shift for more years than I care to remember, I could get to like driving this li'l feller."

"That runs in your family," Deputy Sheriff Brad

Counter replied. "Alice's been dropping hints about how she'd like to take it for a spin."

Contacting Willard Cosset by arrangement after the Watch ended the previous afternoon, Brad had paid him for the information and asked if he would pass the word should Alonzo Nevada make another delivery. Completing their part in the Range Qualification Shoot earlier than anticipated that morning and having nothing urgent demanding their attention, they were going back to Gusher City by a circuitous route. This allowed Cord to drive the blond giant's open-topped, imported M.G. MGB convertible for the first time. They had selected the less direct route, as it did not have the flow of traffic that would be using the freeway. This had been considered advisable because the blond giant had not had the vehicle converted to left-hand drive and his partner was no longer accustomed to changing the gears manually.

"She always did have good taste," Cord drawled.

"Why, sure," Brad agreed, although neither he nor his partner imagined that tragic circumstances would cause him to form a team with Woman Deputy Alice Fayde in the not too distant future.

"Cen-Con to any units in Drayton area!" came an announcement on the two-way radio installed in the car, and their conversation was quickly brought to a close.

"Deputies Cord and Counter by," the blond giant said, scooping up the microphone and making the required answer. "We are two miles west of Drayton. Over."

"Go to the Bergen Pet-Meats Packing Plant," instructed the dispatcher for the Central Control at the Department of Public Safety Building in Gusher City. "We've had a six-two-nine saying there's going to be a protest outside and something more than just shouting and waving banners is in the air."

"Will do," Brad assented, knowing the number quoted

meant the report had come from the local Field Office of
the Federal Bureau of Investigation and was coded from
the numbers in the alphabet of the initials. "Over and
out."

"And *you* wanted to take a nice, quiet drive in the country," Cord sniffed, despite the suggestion having been
made by himself. "I wonder what the banner wavers want
with Bergen's?"

"Animal rights freaks, likely," Brad guessed. "Some of
them are real mean sons of bitches, although they mostly
stick to mailing bombs, or doing their thing when they
won't be seen."

"Well, it's up to *us* to keep the peace," the older deputy
declared. "We'll soon be able to see what's doing. It'll be in
sight once we've topped this rim."

As was predicted, the source of the possible trouble
came into view as the deputies reached the top of the slope
their vehicle was climbing. Just below the rim, the road
they were on joined another somewhat wider one. Although Brad had not been in the area before, he had no
difficulty in locating the Bergen Pet-Meats Packing Plant.
It was the only human habitation within their range of
vision. Composed of half a dozen not too large corrugated
iron buildings, surrounded by a high chain-link fence, there
was nothing impressive about it. Nevertheless, clearly it
was the object of a gathering to protest about its activities,
or perhaps its presence in the area.

Some fifty or so people of various ages, many carrying
placards that could not be read from the deputies' position, were already forming up on the wide road in front of
the closed front main gates. What was more, judging by the
group of men assembled just inside the fence, the owners
were taking measures to protect their property. Whether
by design or chance, the protesters were blocking the road
that descended the steep incline to form an intersection

with the wider one they would have used if they had come from Gusher City.

Already a crew from the local television network had their equipment set up to record what was happening for the evening newscast, and the deputies guessed representatives from the county's two newspapers, especially the "liberal"-oriented *Daily Reflex*, would be present. However, the possibility of media coverage did not particularly interest either of them at that moment. Their sole concern was how to deal with the situation. Nor was reaching a decision helped by there being no sign of other official vehicles around to act as support.

"Hot damn!" Cord swore, removing his gaze from the scene at the foot of the slope. While slowing the M.G., he turned his eyes to where a vehicle topped the rim to their right and, traveling fast, began to go down the slope. Like the packing plant, the vehicle suggested that the owners had a less than munificent financial standing in the area. It was an ex–U.S. Army four-ton, 6 × 6, Diamond T truck with the name BERGEN PET-MEATS PACKING PLANT inscribed in faded white letters upon its grubby, still G.I. "dark earth"–colored sides. "That jasper's sure in a hurry to get to work!"

"*Which* Jasper?" Brad barked, also staring at the vehicle and not caring for the implications of the sight. "There's *nobody* in the cab!"

"We've got to get those protesters out of the way!" the older deputy asserted, pressing the accelerator so the M.G. increased its speed.

"There'll be no time for that," the blond giant estimated. "Their kind won't be willing to listen to two lawmen!"

"You're right," Cord admitted, wishing he and his companion were in civilian clothes and not their uniforms as required by the Range Qualification Shoot they had attended. "What the—?"

"Put us alongside it!" Brad requested, the part question having been caused by the older deputy seeing him unfasten his seat belt. "I'm going to make a stab at getting into the cab!"

"You're *loco*!" Cord declared, but started to do as he was asked.

"Hell," Brad countered—no pun intended—slipping free from the belt. "Fellers do it all the time in movies and television cop shows."

While speaking, the blond giant eased himself upward. By the time he was standing erect, balancing himself against the movement beneath him, the M.G. was ranging alongside the truck. For the first occasion since he had bought it, he wished he had done as the salesman suggested and had had it converted from the British right-hand drive. Having refrained from authorizing the modification meant he was looking into the fortuitously open window of the seat for the passenger and not the driver's seat.

"This'll teach you not to be so goddamned *impatient*," Brad mused, measuring the distance separating the two vehicles with his eyes. Then he raised his voice and continued, "Get going as fast as you can when I jump and try to make those yo-yos move, just in case—!"

"Don't you *dare* have an 'in case'!" the older deputy replied, his deep concern showing under the gruffness of his voice. "And that's an *order*!"

"Yo, *boss*!" the blond giant answered, giving the traditional U.S. Army assent to a command. "I'm going on 'three.' One! Two! THREE!"

Completing the count, Brad placed a foot on the door of the M.G. and, trying not to look down at the surface of the road rushing below him, he thrust himself over the side. Considering the short distance actually involved, hurtling across the intervening space seemed to take a very long time. However, while doing so, he felt gratitude to the manufacturers for having equipped the cab with a sturdy and fairly wide running board, which he believed would make his task just a little easier. Then he arrived at his destination. To the accompaniment of a silent "Thanks!" intended for whoever had left the window open, he thrust his arms through and hooked them over the bottom. An instant later, his feet found the solid metal of the running board and, except for entering the vehicle, he knew he had completed the first part of his task successfully.

"Goddamn it, this time Tom was *right!*" the blond giant breathed, glancing over his shoulder and discovering that his partner was already pulling ahead. Starting to open the door and maneuver himself inside the cab, he went on, "I must have been loco to even think of trying this, and I'll *never* watch another goddamned movie or television 'cop' show!"

The sentiment, uttered to help calm him down, was barely completed before Brad drew himself thankfully inside the vehicle. What he saw while moving across the seat informed him that the empty condition of the cab was no accident. The steering wheel had been jammed by a forked stick and another held the accelerator depressed. However, a glance ahead warned him that he must not waste time pondering over the discovery.

As soon as the blond giant was gripping the steering wheel with one hand, he knocked away the sticks and placed his foot on the liberated accelerator. With that done, he made a very rapid assessment of the situation. Whoever had abandoned the truck must have quit the cab before it reached the top of the rim and, of necessity, had left it in gear. However, this did not do much to lessen the danger. While the engine being in gear had applied some restraint, in addition to the accelerator having been jammed fully down, the weight of the vehicle and its cargo was causing it to build up more speed as it made the descent.

Brad was an excellent driver and, since becoming a deputy, had added to his skill by handling trucks as well as cars and motorcycles over the Department of Public Safety's exacting and demanding Emergency Vehicles Operations Course. Nevertheless, despite having successfully completed the transfer from the M.G., he did not consider his present task to be any sinecure. While they were driving toward their destination, Cord had told him something of the Bergen Pet-Meats Packing Plant. Run on a shoestring budget, it did not compete with the major companies dealing in similar commodities. The majority of its products were shipped into Mexico, where, according to rumor, they were much used for food by the poorer sections of the community instead of being given to dogs and cats. The assertion was never proven, but the Rockabye County Department of Health's inspectors made regular examinations of the plant to ensure that, despite the products used being of a lower quality than was considered acceptable for human consumption, a suitable standard of hygiene was carried out and the goods would at least be safely edible for animals. In spite of this, he doubted whether the company spent much money on maintaining its machinery in top condition. For one thing, even if it had been manufactured since World War II ended, the truck had not come from the production line recently.

While envisaging the difficulties, the blond giant was never a man to be plagued by uncertainties and self-doubt. He knew he must act, and the longer he delayed, the greater grew the chances of failing to carry out his intentions. With that in mind, he eased his foot on the accelerator and used the clutch, then the stick shift, to crash into a lower gear. However, when he began to apply the foot brake tentatively, he received a gratifying surprise. Bearing in mind the shoestring operation of the plant, he had not expected much assistance from the brakes. However, they responded to his manipulation. A moment's thought explained why this was probably the case. A company like Bergen's would know that the eyes of more than just the Health Department were likely to be kept on it. Therefore, as he now realized, they would ensure their vehicles were maintained at a standard that would satisfy inspection by the Highway Patrol or other law enforcement authorities.

Regardless of his gratitude, Brad was all too aware that the danger was still not past. Looking through the fly-splashed windshield, he could see that Cord was already almost at the foot of the slope. What was more, either his partner had contrived to alert the protesters to their peril, or somebody else had seen the truck careering down the slope and beat him to it. Whichever was the reason, discarding their banners, they were hurriedly scattering.

"Now," the blond giant told himself under his breath, noticing with relief that Cord had swung the M.G. aside before bringing it to a stop and was getting out to open the trunk, in which they had placed their hats and nightsticks before leaving the firing range. "All I have to do is stop this son of a bitch without a skid that could roll it over, or hitting the front gates!"

Putting to use all his ability, Brad succeeded in doing as he wished. However, it was a very near thing. The front bumper was only six inches from the gates when his skillful manipulation of the hand and foot brakes slowed and then brought the heavy vehicle to a stop. Letting out his breath in a long whoosh, he listened to something he had never expected to hear—especially when he was wearing his uniform and easily identified as a peace officer—applause and shouts of praise coming from a group of protesters. Waiting for a few seconds to compose himself, he contrived to climb from the cab as if boarding a truck in such a fashion was an everyday occurrence. However, pleasing as the approbation of the protesters was, he considered the expression of relief on his partner's normally impassive face to be far more satisfactory.

"Like you ordered, boss, no 'in case,'" the blond giant drawled, accepting the uniform Stetson and nightstick that Cord had fetched from the M.G. "Do me a favor, though."

"Name it and she's done," the older peace officer replied.

"*Please* don't tell me one of your jokes to show you figure I've done good," Brad requested, such being his partner's way of expressing approbation. Slipping the nightstick into its belt loop and donning his hat while he was speaking, he continued, "That way you'll make me a happy man!"

"Howdy you-all, Mr. Chorley," Deputy Sheriff Tom Cord said, getting down to the business at hand by looking at the stocky, balding middle-aged man in a not too expensive, but neat, business suit and with a pewter belt buckle inscribed "Redneck and Proud of It," who was hurrying toward the main gate. Waving his right hand toward the truck, he went on, "I reckon this is yours."

"It's ours, all right," the manager of the Bergen Pet-Meats Packing Plant confirmed in a Texan's drawl, his florid face showing a mixture of anger and puzzlement. "How the hell did it get back here?"

"Now that's a right smart question," Cord admitted dryly. "And I reckon there's more than you would like to know the answer."

"Where the hell's Solly?" Oscar Chorley demanded, glaring from Deputy Sheriff Brad Counter to the now empty cab. "The driver?"

"He wasn't there when we first saw the heap coming

over the hill," Cord replied. "Fact being, nobody else was either."

"Then where the hell's he got to?" the manager growled.

"Maybe he was told to send the truck down here," one of the protesters yelled, and there was an ugly rumbling of concurrence with the suggestion.

"It'd left here before any of these scum-rades arrived, deputy," Chorley shouted. "And why the hell they've come, I don't know. We *never* use whale meat; it's too goddamned expensive."

"Did you try telling them that?" Cord inquired.

"Their kind never listen, unless it comes direct from Moscow," the manager answered, looking at the protesters with disgust plain on his face. "They've just come to make trouble."

"Could be," Cord admitted, then glanced pointedly at the workmen who were forming a loose half-circle behind Chorley. They were showing signs of being ready to repel any attempts at forcible entry, and judging from the objects they were grasping, some clearly did not intend to restrict their resistance to bare hands. "And you look like you're all set to make some back."

"A man's entitled to protect his home, or place of work," the manager asserted.

"That depends on how he goes about it," Cord answered, wishing he could hear sirens announcing the approach of vehicles ordered as "backup" by Central Control. However, feeling sure the precaution had been taken by the man he was addressing, even though it was not the manager's call that was responsible for himself and his partner arriving, he went on, "You called in for us to come and take care of things, so leave us do it. Which I'll feel a whole heap easier was you to tell those fellers back of you to head inside and get on with their work."

"With only just the two of you here?" Chorley growled,

having no reason to suspect the presence of the deputies was not in response to the telephone call he had told his secretary to make when the protesters began to gather. "All those scum-rades'll come busting in like they was threatening to before you got here."

"My partner and me'll 'tend to them if they do," Cord stated. "And there's more badges on the way. *You* can make the first move at keeping things peaceable by sending those fellers back to work."

"But—!" the manager began, then reconsidered. He was all too aware that his establishment was not held in high regard by the County's authorities, and he had no desire to antagonize a man whose official position could offer numerous opportunities of creating difficulties for him. He was already facing attempts and threats by a labor union seeking to force him to allow the enlistment of the members of his work force whether they wished to do so or not, and, in fact, he felt sure they were responsible for the presence of the protesters. Therefore, he did not also want trouble with the law. "All right, boys. Go on back to work!"

While the conversation had been taking place, the blond giant was looking the crowd of protesters over. They were much what he expected for such a gathering, having the appearance of being the kind of semiprofessional agitators who were always ready to espouse any cause so long as it offered an excuse to create trouble. He was willing to bet that, regardless of their race, they were all products of middle-class–middle-management backgrounds who had "dropped out" because of an inability to compete and who had adopted "causes" to make up for their inadequacies in more productive fields. Although there was the usual leavening of representatives from ethnic "minorities"—a trio of Hispanics, a couple of all too obvious Indians, and a black—present, the rest were white. Almost all of the latter men were long haired, bearded, looked in need of a wash, and wore grubby clothes after the fashion of Philip Turner, and few of the women were any more tidy or presentable.

The banners that were still lying where they had been discarded in the rush to get clear of the approaching truck indicated the reason for the demonstration. Glancing around quickly, Brad read, "Gays Against Whale Killing," "Lesbians Protest the Use of Whale Meat," "Keep Whales, Not Nukes," and other slogans, all dealing with the same theme. However, there were indications that more than just having a peaceful protest assembly had been contemplated. In addition to some of the banners having far thicker wooden handles than was necessary merely to support the slogans, scattered around were several things clearly more suitable as extemporary weapons. Not far from his feet, a steel crowbar for which he could think of no other use lay across a banner inscribed, "Lovers of Peace Demand End to Use of Whale Meat."

One thing became apparent to the blond giant as he was conducting his observations. The crowd was coming together again and, he felt sure, would soon be continuing with their interrupted activities. What was more, while they had shown approbation over the way he had boarded the truck to slow it and give them time to escape, he did not doubt they would revert to their normal hatred of peace officers should they be ordered by his partner to desist.

Watching the first of the protesters starting to retrieve the discarded banners, Brad decided to take what he hoped would prove preventive action. With one of his upbringing and nature, to think was to act. Stepping forward, he bent and picked up the crowbar. Without showing signs of being interested in the actions of the crowd, or noticing they were also watching him, he raised it over his head. Resting it upon the back of his Stetson's wide brim to offer some relief against what he intended, he began to pull at it with his hands. For a few seconds, nothing happened. However, the expression on his almost classically handsome face and whole bearing offered testimony to the great strain he was exerting. Then, to the accompaniment of ripping cloth as the sleeves of his shirt burst open under the pressure of his enormous bulging biceps, and evoking gasps of astonishment from the onlookers, the ends of the bar started to move forward. Nor did he halt his tremendous effort until he had bent the steel until it looked like a big horseshoe. Having accomplished this, he tossed it on the ground and stood with arms akimbo and breathing heavily.

"*Bueno,* Mr. Chorley," Cord drawled in the silence that followed his partner's Herculean display of strength. Although the workmen had stayed to watch, they were now turning to walk away. "You was saying you don't use whale meat?"

"We don't," the manager agreed in an equally carrying tone. "And never have."

"Then you wouldn't mind happen a couple or so of these good folks looked around to see that's so?" the deputy suggested.

"The hell I wouldn—!" Chorley answered, then he gave a shrug. "All right, have a couple of them do it. Only search them first. I don't aim to have them fetching in anything to leave hidden around and get me in dutch with County Health."

"How about it, ladies and gentlemen?" Cord called, turning to the crowd and feeling relieved to hear the wailing of approaching sirens heralding the pending arrival of support. "Will two of you come in and make sure there isn't any whale meat being used?"

"They can go anyplace they want and look through all my books, should they be so inclined—and any of them can remember how to read," the manager declared, glancing to where the television crew were directing their camera and other equipment toward himself and the deputy he was addressing. Wanting to avoid any suggestion that he was unwilling to help avert trouble and to refute the cause of it, but unable to refrain from continuing to show his dislike and distrust of the demonstrators, he went on, "Just so long's they've been *searched* before they come through the gate."

For a moment, even though the television camera was swung toward the crowd, there was no reply. Instead, everybody started to look suggestively at everybody else. Chorley gave a snort that indicated he considered the hesitation to allow the search he had wanted was proof that noxious substances *had* been brought for the purpose of planting in the factory. However, Cord was more inclined to suspect that a desire to avoid being found to be in possession of marijuana, or "harder" narcotics, was the reason for the reluctance to be searched.

"Hell!" the only black member of the crowd said, stepping forward. Tall, well built, and good looking, he was clean, albeit cheaply dressed in keeping with the image of being a member of a "poor and downtrodden" section of society. *"I've* got nothing to hide. How about you, Tom Lindstrom?"

"Or me," declared a tall, slender young white man, also advancing. "I reckon between us, Chekumbia Nyoka, we must have been shaken down at least *six hundred and twenty-nine* times by the pigs without ever once having been caught carrying so much as an asprin."

"See to the searching and go with them, Brad," Cord instructed. "I'll stay out here and wait for the boys from Drayton."

"Yo!" the blond giant assented, lifting his gaze from studying the effect that bending the crowbar had had on his hat and deciding he would have to get it blocked at the shop from which it was purchased before it would return to its original shape. Nothing on his face showed that—like his partner—he had appreciated the significance of the number emphasized by the slender white protester, and he walked forward, saying, "Let's get her done, gents."

Maintaining the excellent cooperation their organization showed to every other law enforcement agency throughout the whole of the country, the local Field Office of the Federal Bureau of Investigation had informed Sheriff Jack Tragg and Chief Phineas Hagen of the Gusher City Police Department that—as elsewhere—they had agents working undercover among the various "protest" movements in the area to ascertain the extent of control being exerted by elements of Communist persuasion. Being in agreement with the objective, neither of the senior local peace officers had raised objections to the FBI's policy of refraining from disclosing the identities of the men involved in the interests of retaining their cover. Instead, both had accepted that the undercover agents would identify themselves if necessary by making some reference to the code numbers and each had informed the men under his command of that code.

Despite realizing he was dealing with two "G-Men," the blond giant also knew that Chorley, the television crew, and men he recognized as working for the two local newspapers were watching him, so he conducted a search that appeared to be thorough, even though he did not put a hand into either's pockets. However, although his external searching located small items on both that he would otherwise have investigated more closely, he made no attempt to do so. Instead, at the conclusion of the search, he stepped back and announced they were "clean." Accepting the report without question or argument, the manager unlocked and opened the front gate to let them enter. Nevertheless, being clearly disinclined to take chances with only one deputy remaining to keep watch over the crowd, he closed and secured it again once they were through.

Before the inspection could be started, the first black and white radio patrol car bearing the insignia identifying it as belonging to the Sheriff's Sub-Office at Drayton arrived. However, instead of keeping the two deputies it carried to help should there be trouble, Cord sent them up the steeply sloping road with instructions to try to find out what had happened to the driver of the truck.

Leading the way toward the nearest building, Chorley told the three young men something of the way in which the packing plant operated. He explained that they carried out some of the slaughtering on the premises and, making it clear he considered the explanation was purely for the benefit of the "protesters," declared this was done in the most humane way possible and the methods employed met with the approval of inspectors from the Society for the Prevention of Cruelty to Animals. He repeated his assertion that no whale meat was ever used because the company considered it cost too much to purchase, saying the last part with relish to annoy his unwanted pair of visitors and—Brad concluded, showing little tact—gave the impression they would do so if the price was lower. When neither commented, he announced that horses were occasionally purchased to supplement cattle, pigs, or sheep as the basic element of the product.

"And, afore you start waving fresh banners," the manager went on, glowering at the white "protester" rather than the black. "They aren't descendants of some that got away from Cortez and've been running wild for generations. It's like the cattle, pigs, and sheep we use, they're the culls which would have been killed by the farmers and ranchers as being useless anyway. All we do is save the carcasses going to waste. We use *all* the meat, fat and lean, in our food and sell the bones and hides."

Having made what he considered to be an essential point, Chorley showed the trio what was happening in the buildings given over to preparing the food, then showed them the filling, labeling, and packing areas where the cans were prepared for shipment. Then he led the way to the largest structure, which stood at the rear of the property and was separated from the rest. Explaining that it was where the animals were slaughtered and butchered, he held open the door. Following them inside, Brad thought Chorley looked disappointed that neither of the "protesters" showed signs of being nauseated by the sights that greeted them.

Although the blond giant did not know it, his guess was correct, and the manager, hoping to produce the desired effect even though the slaughtering was finished, took his visitors to see the carcasses being butchered. As he had claimed, nothing was being wasted. When as much meat as possible had been stripped off by hand, the remains were put into large vats filled with boiling water to remove the rest. With this accomplished, the bones were laid on beds to dry. However, that did not conclude the visit. In another section of the building, the hides of the animals killed that day were being stretched on frames and rubbed down with salt to ensure they dried out.

"Was I to make a guess," Brad remarked after having watched a man starting to work on the nearest hide—which still retained its hair—with more interest than he had shown in the tour until that moment, "I'd say you're not processing beef today."

"Nope," Chorley agreed, attaching no particular significance to the remark and giving an explanation more for the benefit of the "protesters" than the big blond peace officer. "I've bought a bunch of the scrubbiest horses I've ever seen, but they were healthy enough and we're using them. Hell, at the prices we charge, we can't run to porterhouse, nor T-bone steak, and anyways, I reckon horse meat's good as either to feed to dog or cats. It's printed on the label that there's horse meat used."

"Well, gents," Brad drawled, looking once more at the hide that had caught his attention to satisfy himself there was no mistake about the summation he had just formed and that had prompted his question. "I haven't seen any whale meat being used, have you?"

"There doesn't *appear* to be any," Lindstrom admitted, with what sounded like reluctance and annoyance at having been compelled to give a negative answer. Then, behaving as any "liberal" would do under similar circumstances, he went on in a thinly veiled condescending fashion, "Does there, Chekumbia Nyoka?"

"I've not seen any," the black admitted, also sounding disappointed.

"There isn't and there never has been," Chorley stated and then said what the blond giant had hoped he would say when Brad had raised the query. "But, so's you'll know that for sure, come and look over our books."

Taking the peace officer and the two "liberals" to his office, the manager produced a ledger that contained information about the purchases of meat. Feeling sure there would be no reference to whale meat being purchased, even if it should be used, despite the claims made by Chorley, Brad was interested only in the latest entry. Memorizing the source from which the horses had come, he waited impatiently for the "protesters" to "satisfy" themselves that the cause of the demonstration was without foundation. With this done, they returned to the road and Lindstrom made the announcement.

"You know something?" Agent Frank "Chekumbia Nyoka" Williams said to a woman holding a banner inscribed, "Lesbians Protest the Use of Whale Meat," having gone to mingle with the crowd while his partner was speaking. "I think we've been *had*. I heard a couple of the gays saying they'd heard there was going to be a demonstration at Ysabel Air Base and free pot, even fixes, would be handed out. I bet the Anti-Nukes bunch spread the word about there being whale meat here to keep us away and leave all the freebies for themselves."

Moving on, the black repeated his story—giving the woman credit for the claim—to a representative of the Lovers of Peace Demand End to Use of Whale Meat faction. By the time he had spoken with two more groups, the story was being spread and, because they distrusted everybody, even their own kind, knowing they would behave in a similar fashion given the opportunity, it produced the desired effect. Claiming there was no need to continue the protest, the recipients of the false information drifted to their vehicles and drove away.

"Well," Cord remarked to Brad, watching the last of the protesters leaving. "They sure went easy and quiet."

"It's all done by kindness and understanding," the blond giant replied, suspecting that the black FBI undercover agent had helped organize the departure. "Anyways, we've been lucky here. Let's hope we're just as lucky the next time Tricky Al comes over the great, gray-green and greasy Rio Grande."

"You reckon he will?" the older deputy inquired.

"Sure," Brad answered. "Unless finding us waiting scares him off."

"It never has before," Cord remarked, studying his partner in a speculative fashion. "How come you're still interested in him?"

"It's only a feeling I've got, mind," the blond giant admitted. "But I reckon I know what he was smuggling in."

"Well, it went easy like they said it would," Tomas Santiago remarked, riding with his nominal employer toward a small ranch house in the rolling open scrub-covered country a couple of miles outside Gusher City.

"*They* don't have to take the risks," Alonzo "Tricky Al" Nevada replied. "If I'd had my way, I'd have waited for at least a couple of weeks before making another run."

"The pigs didn't find anything last time," Santiago pointed out. "And that stupid bunch of *gringo* do-gooders who're fronting for us have made sure they don't search like they did before."

"*That's* what worries me," the smuggler asserted. "The Customs officers over here don't usually give up so easy, nor Jack Tragg's boys, come to that."

"We've got them all licked," Santiago claimed.

"That's how it *looks*," Nevada admitted, then he waved a hand to the horses they were leading, which no longer carried loads on the pack saddles. "But I won't be sorry when we're paid for this bunch and are back into Mexico."

Being a compulsive gambler with a tendency toward such disastrous habits as betting on several horses in each race of a track meet, drawing to inside straights at poker, and accepting the most outrageous "sucker bets" when shooting craps, Nevada never contrived to save much of the money he made as a smuggler. In fact, added to his unwise tactics, a recent run of exceptionally bad luck had caused him to sign several IOU's to cover his losses. Wondering how he could clear his indebtedness, and being aware that failure to do so would prove extremely painful, he had been contacted by the man to whom he owed the money. He was told his services were required to help in a deal upon which the owners of the game were engaged. They had obtained a number of horses, for which there was no market in Mexico, and wanted them delivered to the United States without the formality of legal entry.

Thinking the matter over, spurred on by the inducement of getting out of debt, Nevada had come up with a scheme.

Contacting the Society for Encouraging the Use of Energy-Conserving Transport, whom he had heard of and whom he had planned to use in another venture, he had said he wanted to help out the poor manufacturers of curios made in Mexico by delivering their products to the more lucrative markets offered by the United States, and that it was his intention to do so by using a train of packhorses instead of trucks. The organizers had agreed to give their assistance to the project and, with their help, he had obtained all the necessary permits for exporting and importing the consignment.

Stating there were far too many horses for a single delivery, Nevada had estimated the greatest number he considered could be handled and his views had been accepted. However, he had been far from enamored by the insistence of his employers and the Society that he be accompanied by Santiago and Phillip Purser to look after their respective interests. Given no choice in the matter, he had decided to make the best of the situation by using them instead of hiring more competent assistance. Having his mare and the three mules trained to follow her would allow him to deal with the majority of the horses, and he had felt sure the pair could cope with the rest. Except for the apparently accidental dumping of Purser from the startled horse, which he had regarded as being most amusing, his confidence had been justified.

In spite of having been surprised by the appearance of the deputies from the Rockabye County Sheriff's Office on the banks of the Rio Grande, Nevada was satisfied he had convinced them he was engaged upon an unorthodox, but completely legal, transportation of cheap "tourist junk." Having delivered the consignment to its destination and left Purser behind, he and Santiago had made their way by a circuitous route to the ranch they were once again approaching. Arriving there and placing the horses in a corral, they had loaded the pack saddles into a truck. While Santiago took it back to Mexico on the main road, Nevada had returned with his mare and the mules by the route he had used to reach Texas.

While the smuggler had known his indebtedness would not be considered clear until all the horses were delivered, he had been far from pleased to learn how quickly his employers expected him to complete the assignment. His plea to leave the next delivery for longer than the week he was given had been refused and, on being told he must do as he was told, he had yielded to the inevitable. Claiming the first consignment had proved so lucrative that another was to be dispatched, he had once again asked for and received the support of the Society in obtaining the necessary documentation. Although wishing they had not insisted upon informing the United States Customs and Rockabye County Sheriff's Office of the event, he was in fact pleased by the arrangement of the former to send men to examine the consignment before it left Mexico. In addition to this, he was relieved to be told the Society did not consider it necessary to send along a representative.

Nevertheless, despite everything having gone smoothly, the smuggler was ill at ease.

"There you are, *senor*," Alonzo Nevada said, with the "simple Mexican *peon*" accent he generally employed when talking to *gringos*, closing the gate after the last of the animals had gone by him. "All safe and sound in your corral. It is a good night's work, I think."

"Good enough," replied the burly American who was in charge of the ranch.

"Then I will take my money and go," the smuggler declared, having no liking for the man. "My cousin Tomas can fetch the saddles like last time."

"I'll pay you off right away," the American promised,

reaching inside his jacket with his right hand. However, it was not money he brought out. Starting to turn the revolver he produced into line, he went on, "And for k—!"

The words came to an end as there was a brilliant flash of light from alongside a clump of bushes about thirty feet away!

"Peace officers here!" a voice bellowed an instant later, and a whistle shrilled loudly from the same place.

An explosive profanity burst out of the white man's mouth, being echoed by one in Spanish from Santiago. Turning their gaze in the direction from which the interruption had originated, they saw two figures in the uniforms of deputies from the Rockabye County Sheriff's Office standing alongside the bushes. The shorter was holding a U.S.M.1 carbine, but the other had nothing more lethal than a camera with a flashgun attached in his left hand and a whistle in the right. What was more, although at a considerable distance away, they heard the sound of vehicles being started and knew more peace officers would soon be converging upon the ranch.

"Get the pig bastards!" the white man yelled, but kept his own weapon directed at Nevada.

Taking in the situation, Deputy Sheriff Tom Cord reacted with speed and precision. Snapping the butt of the carbine to his shoulder, he lined the sights and squeezed the trigger before the revolver could be fired at the smuggler. Taken in the shoulder by the bullet, the burly man spun around with the weapon flying from his grasp and began to bellow, in a pain-filled voice, that he surrendered. However, despite Nevada having been saved from the American, the danger to him was not at an end. What was more, the lives of Cord and his companion were at risk. Two more white men had been helping with the unsaddling of the horses and were running to where they had left a pump-action shotgun and a rifle leaning against the side of the corral.

Having no need of the advice, Santiago was already reaching for the revolver that the smuggler had prevented him from drawing on the previous occasion when they had been challenged by the same pair of peace officers. He had no doubt that Nevada, who—despite his habit of never carrying a gun when working—was known to be very dangerous if crossed, would take steps to repay him for his part in the treachery if allowed to survive. Being determined to ensure this did not happen, he was relying upon the two *gringos* to keep the peace officers occupied while he looked after himself. What was more, if the *gringos'* presence was not suspected by the deputies, they might provide a means for him to escape before the backup units, which the blast on the whistle had summoned, could arrive on the scene.

"Watch those two by the corral!" Nevada yelled as Santiago was drawing his conclusions, being thankful for the intervention even though he knew it was almost certain to end with a prison term for him.

Grateful as Cord and Deputy Sheriff Brad Counter were for the warning, it was not required. Having taken up their positions shortly after nightfall, they had been watching everything that happened. However, while knowing the two men were nearby and had access to potent weapons, they realized the smuggler was still in danger and, as he was in all probability adhering to his policy of being unarmed when running contraband, he could do nothing to defend himself. Nor did either believe he would not need their assistance. Checking with the commanding officer of the Mexican *Guardia Rurales* operating across the Rio Grande in the area opposite Rockabye County, they had learned Santiago was not related to the smuggler and, even though no convictions had been achieved against him, he had a reputation for being a ruthless killer. Concluding he wished to protect himself against reprisals for his part in the betrayal, they decided he meant to kill Nevada and leave the two Americans to look after themselves.

As Captain Eugenio Machados had warned when Cord spoke with him on the telephone, Santiago was fast with a gun.

Fortunately for Nevada, so was Brad Counter.

What was more, the blond giant was carrying his weapon in a rig that allowed far greater speed than the shoulder holster from which the Mexican was starting to extract the revolver.

"*Them*, Tom!" Brad snapped, allowing the camera and whistle to drop from his hands, the former being on a strap around his neck and the latter still attached to its chain.

Saying just two words and relying upon his partner to realize what they meant, the blond giant set his weight on feet spread approximately to the width of his broad shoulders and bent his legs a little. Inclining his torso slightly to the rear, he flexed his right hand and sent it flashing toward his hip. As his thumb and the other three fingers enfolded the butt of the Colt Government Model of 1911 automatic pistol, which had "combat grips" shaped to ensure he took hold in the same manner every time he started a draw, his forefinger hooked beneath the long tang of the "fly-off" safety strap. Being held under tension, on the press stud being opened, the protective device flew away from the hammer over which it had been looped. Sweeping the gun from the tiny holster, although his thumb rested upon the enlarged manual safety catch, he refrained from pushing it down and kept his forefinger outside the trigger guard until the barrel was clear of leather and pointing away from him.

Such was the skill Brad had acquired that, in around a quarter of a second after his hand's first movement, the

pistol was speed-rocked from the combat bikini rig and
bellowed out. Although the distance separating him from
his objective was somewhat longer than considered suitable for such a method, time did not allow him to attain a
more effective position. Instead, he squeezed the trigger
while aiming by instinctive alignment and at waist level.
Luck, combined with the ability that made him a "sixteen-
dollar shooter," caused the ejected lead to fly where it was
intended. Struck in the center of the chest with a .45-cali-
ber bullet shaped like a truncated cone and powered by a
hand-loaded cartridge that gave it an even greater potential than the issue variety, Santiago reeled backward. Only
just clear of his jacket, the revolver dropped from his hand
and he followed it down.

Justifying his partner's confidence, Cord had known
what was meant by the two words. Swinging the carbine
around, he selected the man he considered to be the more
dangerous of the pair. Nor was he a moment too soon.
Even more so than in Brad's case, sheer chance rather than
a deliberate aim caused the bullet he dispatched to strike
the barrel of the shotgun that was already being pointed
toward them. Nevertheless, the hit proved just as effective
as if it had reached its intended mark. Deflected upward,
but only just enough, the barrel sent its charge of buckshot
hissing close over the deputies' heads. Having the weapon
knocked from his hands, the impact numbing and rendering them inoperative, the man joined his boss in shouting
he was through.

Nor did the last of the Americans fare any better. Startled by the less than satisfactory way in which the situation
was developing, from his point of view, he hesitated instead of deciding immediately what action was best suited
to his needs. The matter was taken from his hands in no
uncertain fashion. As soon as he had fired at Santiago,
using the recoil kick of the big automatic to help, Brad

raised it with his left hand joining the right on the butt. Holding it at arm's length and shoulder height, in the combat shooting posture perfected by Sheriff Jack Weaver of Lancaster, California, he aligned the improved sights fitted to the top of the barrel. Time did not allow him to take as careful aim as he would have preferred. Nevertheless, how effective the Weaver stance could be in expert hands was proved by the bullet Brad turned loose just grazing the ear of the man at whom it was aimed. Startled by the eerie *splat* sound from the closely passing lead and noticing the carbine was also being turned his way, he hurriedly threw the rifle aside and thrust both hands into the air.

"I know I shouldn't be, *senores,*" Alonzo Nevada remarked as the first of the backup vehicles came into view and approached rapidly with its siren wailing. On this occasion, his English was that of an educated man well versed in its use. "But I'm *very* pleased to see you."

"You can thank my *amigo* for us being here," Deputy Sheriff Tom Cord answered without taking his attention from the other men.

"Hell, it was dumb luck on my part," Deputy Sheriff Brad Counter asserted, also keeping the captives under observation. "And a coincidence you'd never believe if you read it in a book. You remember that ugly yellowish and white blotched crowbait Purser was riding?"

"It was hard to forget," the smuggler replied. "I've never before seen a horse that color."

"Or me, although I'm grateful I saw that one," the blond giant declared. "Well, we were out at the Bergen Pet-Meats Packing Plant handling a squeal and I saw its hide being salted down. I found out where it had come from and, when the Customs let us know you were fetching over another shipment of those 'recent antiques,' we reckoned it would be worthwhile staking this place out."

"And it was, for my sake," Nevada declared. "I didn't think they'd decided my services were no longer necessary, so I'm not sorry you were here to save me. What a pity, though. It was such a good game."

"You're telling me," Cord drawled. "Hell, except for Brad coming up with the answer, the last thing we'd have suspected you of smuggling in was *horses*."

PART THREE

SERGEANT RANSE SMITH,
COMPANY "Z," TEXAS RANGERS
In
PERSONA NON GRATA

"Your stoolie was right, Ben," Lieutenant Victorio Bianco said, looking through the window of the Packard Super Eight sedan that had been selected by the man behind the steering wheel as being sufficiently in keeping with the surroundings to pass unnoticed among the other vehicles in the parking lot of the North Dallas Golf and Country Club. "It is Big Frankie Wright from out of Philly. I'm sorry we couldn't send you a mug sheet with photographs and fingerprints, but we've never been able to get him on anything to let us set one up."

There was nothing about the outer appearance of the vehicle or its two occupants to suggest they were peace officers engaged upon a surveillance intended to allow the speaker to identify the man indicated by the driver.

About five foot nine and slim, Bianco had glossy black hair slicked straight back above handsome olive-skinned features and he wore dapper attire in the latest Eastern fashion. Despite looking like a gigolo from a high-class dance hall, he was a lieutenant of the Philadelphia Police Department with a reputation for tough and incorruptible competence.

About three inches taller, with the lean build of one still engaged in strenuous activities, Major Benson Tragg might have been a prosperous rancher in town on business. In fact, although he owned a ranch and spent what time he could there, he was a major of the Texas Rangers. His lightweight brown suit was Western in cut and the calf-high brown riding boots, which he wore inside the legs of his trousers, had the high heels and sharp toes still favored by cowhands. However, excellent though the fit otherwise was, his tailor had not been entirely successful when making the jacket in concealing the bulge of a short-barreled and heavy-caliber Colt revolver holstered butt forward on the left side of his waist belt.

"It happens," Tragg drawled philosophically, his accent that of a native-born Texan. Knowing the information had come indirectly from Hogan Turtle, the current head of a family whose connections with lawbreaking in Texas went back to the days before independence was won from Mexican domination, he contrived to refrain from showing the amusement he felt over hearing its source described as a "stoolie." "Only I think 'Shorty' would be closer to it if he didn't have those built-up heels and soles on his shoes. How come the 'Big Frankie'?"

"You know the blown-up ego all his kind have," Bianco replied, also eyeing the man under discussion in a less than flattering fashion. "He likes to think nobody notices how short he is and folks who know him go along with it if they want to keep a safe skin. We wondered where he and some of his boys had gone when they disappeared after Chief Ballinger started the big cleanup in Philly. Then you sent word they'd all moved down here to Big D."

"I figured Sam would like to know," Tragg admitted,

having been in contact by telephone with Chief of Police Samuel Ballinger—a friend of long standing—in Philadelphia as soon as he received the news from Turtle. "The DPD've located the Talker, Dirty Kev Bradshaw and some of the others, but they've been so well behaved since they hit town there's nothing to pull them in for. What's more, so far as the local badges know, except for the Talker meeting up with him a couple of times and Bradshaw dogging him around at a distance 'most everywhere he goes, the rest haven't been near him and he's living all clean and respectable among the rich folks."

"He *always* did," Bianco asserted grimly. "Even though we know how close he came to running Philly the way the mobs have got Chicago sewn up, we haven't been able to nail him for so much as a parking ticket. No matter what his game is, and I'm *certain* he has one, it'll be the same down here."

"That's why we're taking a hand," Tragg stated, being in command of the elite—albeit unknown outside a very small circle of high-ranking officials in the State Legislature—Company "Z" of the Texas Rangers. "We're going to find some way we can say, 'Mr. Philo Anstruther, we know that's just a summer name and you're Big Frankie Wright from Philadelphia, so you and your boys're persona non grata hereabouts, which means we've got enough homegrown owlhoots and you'd best get the hell out of Texas.' "

"I was hoping you'd be able to do more than just that."

"We'll surely try. Don't you have anything at all on Wright?"

"Not a thing, like I said," the Lieutenant confessed. "He's always covered his tracks too well. But we've got plenty on some of the other members of his mob. Tongues started wagging when word got out that Big Frankie and his top boys had left town. That's why I'm here, to put the arm on them and have them extradited back to Philly for trial. Even if we can't get their boss, we'll have them."

"Why sure," Tragg said. "But, happen you go along with us, we might be able to do a mite more than that."

"I'd be all for it!" Bianco enthused, hoping against hope that the "mite more" would include some way of arresting and convicting Wright. "What do you have in mind?"

"Stirring things up a mite for his boys," Tragg replied. "Get them wondering what the hell's going on. I've told Sam something of what we have in mind, and he agrees there's no rush for you to start putting the arm on them, so you can relax and take yourself a vacation."

"I won't argue about *that*," the Lieutenant said with a grin. "What I've seen so far, Dallas looks like it could be an interesting place."

"It *could* be," the Major conceded. "Except you'll be staying on a friend's ranch out of town and won't be coming in until you're needed."

"I should've known the Chief wouldn't be handing out vacations that easy," Bianco sighed. "When do you start with whatever we've got in mind?"

"It's started already," the Major declared.

"You look annoyed, Talker," Francis Wright remarked in his cultured Chicago accent, having glanced around to make sure there was nobody else in the locker room of the North Dallas Golf and Country Club to hear what he was saying.

Although they were the two leading members of the same gang, there was a great contrast in the appearances of the speaker and the man to whom the words were directed.

As Major Benson Tragg had intimated, even with the assistance of his two-toned shoes' extra-thick soles and heels, Wright was of no more than middle height. What had formerly been a stocky and powerful body had run to fat as the result of overindulgence in luxurious living. Black-haired, albeit going bald, his sallow and somewhat porcine features were suggestive of a libertine, in spite of a shrewd glint in his deep-set eyes. However, although he had been just that in his younger days, since rising to power in Philadelphia, his life had been far more innocent than that of his companion.

Close to six feet, despite having a bulky body clearly gone to seed as a result of his licentious habits, Michael "the Talker" Buffong was a far more imposing physical specimen. Also in his late forties, he had a full head of white hair framing a still good-looking face. A former attorney disbarred for malpractice, even dressed casually for the golf game he had just concluded, he gave the impression of being very wealthy and distinguished, which was a most useful asset to him in his capacity of contact man for the gang. There were several women who had discovered too late his true unsavory nature and the realization had cost one of them her life.

"I'll say I'm *annoyed*!" the Talker agreed in his Back Bay Bostonian tones, slamming down his right spiked golf shoe and starting to unlace the other. "I've just been *rooked*!"

"You?" Wright grunted, knowing his associate to be something of an expert where taking an unfair advantage when playing golf was concerned. "How come?"

"I took on a young man who looked rich enough to make it worth my while," Buffong replied. "He looked like a pigeon and *said* he played off a ten handicap. Goddamn it, if he was more than a *five,* then I'm a—."

"What did you say you played off?" the gang leader asked, as the words died away due to an inability to think of a suitable simile.

"I said I was ten as well," the Talker replied sullenly, having been warned by his boss against being too blatant over cheating. "We were playing for a hundred bucks nassau, with an automatic press on the back. I'd taken the front nine by a hole, but he pulled back when he found out I'd been playing the wrong ball by mistake and we were all square on the seventeenth with only the long par five left to play. He said we should have a hundred dollars on it as well as the nassau to make the game interesting. When I pretended to hesitate, he told me he'd give me two shots on the hole if I'd give him a free throw and, even though I didn't know what he meant, I agreed."

"So how come you lost?" the gang leader inquired, realizing the advantage offered by the terms despite also being ignorant of what a "free throw" entailed.

"We were both on the green in three," the Talker explained, his tone and expression bitter. "And I said, 'Well, I've two shots up on you to get her in the cup for game.' He said, 'Sure, but I still have to have my free throw.' And damned if he didn't pick up my ball and throw it into that son-of-a-bitching deep sand trap to the left of the green!"

"What'd you do about that?" Wright inquired, after laughing and deciding to use the ploy some time.

"What the hell could I do?" Buffong snarled. "It took me four to get out of the sand and three putts. He went down in *two*. So I paid him off, but I'll be damned if he's going to get away with it. I'll have the check stop—"

"The hell you will!" the gang leader interrupted coldly. "I've told you before that I don't want you or any of the other boys doing *anything* to draw attention to yourselves. If you stop it, he'll complain to the Committee and, if he's as smart as I reckon he must be, he could tell them about the tricks you pulled. So let it ride."

"Whatever you say," the Talker acceded with bad grace, knowing there was no point in denying he had employed unfair tactics during the game. "Are you playing today?"

"Sure," Wright confirmed, and his voice took on a smug timbre. "With Judge Robespierre."

"Hell," Buffong grunted, giving no indication of being impressed. "By all accounts, he's the straightest and most incorruptible judge in Texas."

"Don't I know it?" Wright answered. "And that's the reason I'm playing with him. I figure knowing law-abiding folks like him and the others I mix with could come in real useful in a pinch." Then, adopting the air of considering the matter closed and wanting to deal with more important issues, he inquired, "How're you getting on?"

"There's no change. I can't get to *anybody.*"

"Don't tell me everybody in this goddamned burg is *honest*?"

"No, but the ones who aren't have already tied up with Hogan Turtle and they aren't willing to run the risk of breaking with him."

"I knew there was always that chance," Wright asserted. "But you said we'd only need *one* on the take from us and there'd soon be more of them come running."

"That's the way it was in Philly," Buffong reminded, refraining from pointing out that the suppositions with regard to Dallas had been drawn by his boss. "Only, I'm damned if I've been able to connect with him so far."

"Keep trying," Wright ordered. "And there's another thing. Dirty Kev keeps following me everyplace. Tell him this isn't Philly and I don't need a torpedo riding around after me."

"You know Dirty," the Talker answered. "He always followed you in Philly, and once he gets an idea in his head, it's hard to move. Anyway, I'll pass him the word."

"Don't just pass him the word!" Wright corrected, making it a policy never to address any other member of his gang personally and only meeting his second in command for short periods in places like the locker room where they were unlikely to attract attention if seen together. All other communication between them was over the telephone. "You see he *quits*!"

"Whatever you say, Frankie," Buffong assented.

Despite the assurance, the Talker had no intention of carrying it out. He had never been particularly enamored of the way in which his leader ran things. It had been sufficiently annoying when everything was going well in Philadelphia, but he considered the situation had changed radically since they arrived in Texas. He never forgot that, in addition to living in a very expensive and luxurious apartment—while the rest of the gang, Buffong included, occupied less lavish accommodation on the grounds of there being a need to economize until taking over the town—Wright alone had access to the nine hundred thousand dollars salvaged from their loot when they were compelled to flee from their previous haunts. Therefore, instead of doing as he was ordered, he intended to warn Kevin "Dirty Kev" Bradshaw—the enforcer for the gang—to be more circumspect while continuing the surveillance.

"That's *him* just coming in!" the Talker snarled, glancing toward the door leading to the course.

"Don't let him see us together!" Wright ordered. "I might have a chance to play him and get your money back!"

Paying no attention to the bitter scowl directed his way by Michael Buffong before stalking angrily toward the entrance to the showers, Francis Wright looked with interest at the man who entered the locker room. One glance was all he needed to know about why the Talker had not raised any physical objection to the trick that had been played on him. He was willing to admit that he would have shown similar restraint under the circumstances.

A good six feet three in height, with golden blond hair

and exceptionally handsome features, the newcomer was in his early twenties and had a muscular development that was well beyond the average. What was more, despite his size and obvious strength, he carried himself lightly and looked capable of moving very fast should the need arise. Glancing at his expensive-looking gold wristwatch, he went and opened a locker. Having taken off his short-sleeved sports shirt and shoes, instead of going to the shower room, he picked up a towel from the bench and began to dry his massive torso. Then he donned a white silk shirt, a yellow cravat of the same material, gray flannel slacks and high-heeled, sharp-toed black Western boots. However, what happened next caused the watching gang leader to take an even greater interest in him. Removing an open-fronted spring-retention shoulder holster carrying a large revolver from the locker, he donned it without making any attempt to avoid being seen doing so. With it in position, he put on a black blazer with a badge of some kind attached to the left breast pocket and, placing the attire he had removed into the locker, strolled out of the room.

A pensive expression came to Wright's face. Although Dallas was more lax about such matters than Philadelphia would have been, for the young man to be so blatant in strapping on a gun implied he must be a peace officer of some kind. The gang leader considered any "badge" who wore such obviously costly attire and belonged to an expensive establishment like the North Dallas Golf and Country Club was worthy of closer study. What was more, the way he had taken the Talker for a fair sum of money suggested he was lacking in scruples and getting to know him better might prove beneficial.

" 'Scuse me, Mr. Anstruther," one of the club's colored pages said, coming up as the gang leader was deciding to tell Buffong to renew the young man's acquaintance. "Judge Robespierre's done called on the telephone and says he powerful sorry, but he can't make the game with you 'count of something's come up."

Grunting noncommittally, Wright changed his mind. Instead of waiting for the Talker to return from the showers, he went into the dining room. Pausing at the door, he saw the young man was sitting at a table and, wondering how he could begin a conversation, he walked forward. Before he arrived, he was forestalled by seeing Symonds, the headwaiter, going to the blond giant holding a letter with a bank heading to which a check was attached.

"I'm sorry, *sir*," Symonds said in a low voice that nevertheless reached Wright's ears. "But I've been informed by the Management Committee that we can't allow you to sign for any more meals or drinks until this check which came back from the bank has been cleared."

"Then I'll pay *cash*," the blond giant stated, but he looked embarrassed as he reached toward his inside right breast pocket. "I don't have the money with me, but you can cash this check I've been given and cover my tab."

"That's against the Club's rules, I'm afraid, sir," the headwaiter replied.

"Symonds," Wright called, realizing he was being given exactly the opportunity he desired and striding forward. A young peace officer living beyond his means could prove susceptible to bribery and provide the "rotten apple" necessary to persuade others to change their allegiance from Hogan Turtle to his gang. Normally, he would have left such negotiations to Buffong. However, he had noticed that a less respectful attitude had arisen from his second in command since their arrival in Dallas, and he decided that a demonstration of success where the Talker had failed could prove sufficient to reestablish the status quo between them. "Judge Robespierre can't keep our appointment and I hate eating alone. Perhaps this young gentleman might care to join me."

"I'd be pleased to, sir," the blond giant declared without hesitation or embarrassment. His voice was that of a Texan from humbler circumstances than was suggested by his clothes and surroundings. "The name's Longley, William A. Longley, but my *amigos* call me 'Bad Bill.'"

"I'm pleased to have your company, Mr. Longley," Wright asserted after he had introduced himself by his alias to his guest and, having taken the order for their meal, the headwaiter had departed. "And more so since I know how poorly you police officers are paid."

"Poor's the word for it," the big young Texan drawled wryly. "But how'd you guess I was a badge?"

"I saw you strapping on your gun in the locker room," the gang leader explained. "And, even though we're in Texas, that suggested you were a lawman of some kind."

"The suggestion's right, sir," the blond giant confirmed. "I'm a detective and work out of Headquarters."

"Have you been a member here for long?" the gang leader asked, seeing the badge on the blazer was not that of the North Dallas Golf and Country Club.

"I'm not a member," the Texan corrected. "But a gent who is lets me play as his guest because I did him a couple of favors."

"Was that who you were playing with this morning?"

"Nope. Some jasper from up north tried to take me for a sucker, but got trimmed down a mite instead."

The food arrived and, while eating it, Wright was given a description of the tricks pulled by Buffong in attempting to win the game and those used by the blond giant to counter them. The gang leader bellowed with genuinely appreciative laughter on learning how his guest had evened the score by having contrived to change the Talker's ball when taking it from the cup on the sixteenth green and, this having gone unnoticed, had won the next hole by default. However, while amused by the thought of the Talker having been beaten by a better trickster, nothing Wright had heard caused him to revise his opinion that he had met a young peace officer whose honesty was questionable and who might be open to corruption where duty was concerned.

"Didn't I see you out at the racetrack a couple of days back?" the gang leader inquired, noticing no mention was made of the trick that won the game for his guest and refraining from raising the matter. Receiving an answer in the affirmative, he went on, "That was quite a good-looking girl you had with you."

"Good-looking's the word," the blond giant admitted. "And damned *expensive.*"

"She looked as if she might be," the gang leader commented, then changed the subject. "By the Lord, they serve good food here."

The conversation became more general while the meal continued. However, so engrossed had Wright become in his guest and prospective candidate for the sought-after "rotten apple in the barrel" that he did not notice Buffong was watching them from a table at the other side of the room. While having an after-lunch cocktail, served as "tea" in a cup to avoid a too blatantly obvious flouting of the Prohibition laws, Wright mentioned he had received a traffic ticket on his way home from the racetrack and waited to see if the unspoken hint was accepted. However, nothing happened until he and the blond giant were walking toward the front entrance.

"I'll see to it for you, Mr. Anstruther," the young man drawled in a confidential fashion that nevertheless was just loud enough for Buffong to hear. "And don't worry. Nobody'll know you told me."

The Talker had not been able to listen to what was said while the pair were at their table, so he had no idea what caused the cryptic comment. Nor had his attempt to learn more proved successful. The waiter, asked for information, supplied the Texan's name, but disclaimed all knowledge of what his occupation might be. Therefore, at that moment, Buffong suspected his boss of nothing more than having selected his opponent in the unsatisfactory golf game as a guest for lunch in order to antagonize him.

The belief continued until the Talker received a telephone call from Bradshaw at six o'clock that evening.

"They've put the arm on Phil the Weasel!" the enforcer announced without preamble.

"What's he been up to?" Buffong demanded, sharing Wright's desire to avoid having attention drawn to the presence of the gang in Dallas.

"He's not been up to *anything* here," Bradshaw stated. "They've pulled him in for that fur heist in May and're holding him until the cops in Philly can get papers for extradition."

"Do they have enough to hold him for that?" the Talker asked.

"I'll say they do," the enforcer asserted. "The mouth-piece I sent down to try to get him sprung says they know where to find the truck the Weasel and his boys used, the route they took going to the warehouse and coming away, who else was in on it and enough more to make the nab stick. Hell, who could've spilled all that?"

"There aren't many," Buffong assessed pensively.

"You'd best tell the boss what's happened," Bradshaw suggested. "I reckon, even with all the fancy new friends he's making, he'll want to know."

"I suppose he will," the Talker agreed, sensing the enforcer was sharing his misgivings over the way things were going in Dallas. Hanging up, he dialed the number of Wright's apartment and, having delivered the news, went on, "What shall we do?"

"Tell the Weasel to keep his mouth shut while I figure

out a way to get him turned loose," the gang leader ordered. "The first thing, though, is to find out who did the squealing."

"How can we do that?" Buffong inquired, having been giving the same subject consideration and arrived at a worrying conclusion.

"I'll see if Longley can get to know for us."

"Longley?"

"Sure. Don't tell me you've forgotten the young feller who took you in the golf game this morning?"

"I'm not likely to forget him," Buffong said bitterly. "But he told me he was in the oil business. So how can he help?"

"Because the only connection he's got with the oil business is putting some on his gun," Wright explained, and his voice took on a smugly self-satisfied timbre. "He's a dick working out of Headquarters here in town. What's more, he's the rotten apple in the barrel you couldn't find."

Watching his boss approaching between the two lines of cars in the parking lot of the Banyan Club, accompanied by an attractive red-haired girl whose "flapper" attire set off a much better-developed figure than was currently considered the height of fashion, Kevin "Dirty Kev" Bradshaw was filled with resentment and suspicion.

Just under six feet in height, thickset and powerfully built, the enforcer had a face with a muddy complexion—responsible for his sobriquet—which was not improved by a jagged scar down his left cheek. He was dressed in the snap-brimmed gray-fedora hat, three-piece pin-striped suit —the jacket having extra-wide lapels and well-padded shoulders—and other attire made popular by gangsters in Chicago. However, already his expensive and formerly immaculate clothes were showing signs of much wear, indicative of his greatly changed circumstances.

Since arriving in Dallas, like the other eight members of the gang who had fled with Francis Wright, Bradshaw had been compelled to accept far less affluent conditions than those to which he had grown accustomed while they were running things around Philadelphia. Because the sum was far lower than he had grown used to receiving, it had become increasingly irksome to exist upon the money doled out to them through the Talker. Nor could they supplement it in their new location as they had been able to previously. No longer could they go into a bar, restaurant, or shop, and expect service without payment because they were known to be Big Frankie's "top boys." Instead, they were reduced to paying cash for every purchase and were barred from doing anything illegal to augment their finances. While they accepted that the Talker required a better standard of living, in order to acquire the opportunity to make the required contacts for them to start operating again, they were less enamored of their boss still indulging in his tastes for a luxurious existence and also his insistence on not dealing with them personally.

Nor was the situation improved by the latest news to have reached Bradshaw. For the fourth time in as many days, a member of the gang had been arrested for a crime committed before their enforced departure and was being held for extradition to Philadelphia. What was more, each of them was picked up within a couple hours of the enforcer having seen his boss in conversation with the big blond peace officer. Despite having heard the explanation that the Texan was the "rotten apple in the barrel" sought as a prelude to taking over the town, Bradshaw, prompted by hints from the Talker, was becoming increasingly suspicious of the reason for the meetings.

Like Michael Buffong and the rest of the gang, Bradshaw never forgot that Wright alone knew where the money brought from Philadelphia was located. That, rather than believing his services as a bodyguard might be needed, was the reason he had continued to follow his boss since coming to Dallas. Therefore, despite having been told he must quit, he had done as the Talker suggested and kept up the observation without letting himself be detected by Wright.

That evening, Big Frankie had collected the blond giant and the girl from an apartment in downtown Dallas and had brought them to this expensive nightclub. It was the sort of place Bradshaw had frequented in Philadelphia, and he was annoyed that his financial condition was insufficient for him to follow them inside. Instead, he had been compelled to remain in his car and wait for them to come out. To help pass the time, he had smoked a succession of cigarettes made from marijuana and these always had an adverse effect upon his temper and judgment. By the time his boss and the girl put in their appearance, he had worked himself into a state of anger that overrode every other consideration. He did not even wonder where the big Texan might be. Instead, thrusting himself from the car, he lurched toward the couple.

"Who's it to be this time, Frankie?" the enforcer snarled.

"What the—?" Wright began, as he and the girl came to a halt. Peering through the gloom, he recognized the speaker and revised his first assumption that a holdup was contemplated. Starting to move forward and trying to prevent his seething anger from being noticed by his companion, he went on, "You'd best go ho—!"

"Don't try to brush me off, you bastard!" Bradshaw warned, shooting out his left hand to catch his boss by the arm. "Every time you—!"

Before the words ended, there was a dramatic interruption.

Rising from behind and vaulting across the hood of the

nearest car, the big Texan continued to move with a surprising speed for one of his size and bulk. Releasing
Wright, the enforcer let out a profanity and sent his right
hand under the left side of his jacket. The movement was
duplicated at an even greater speed by the blond giant.
Twisting the big British-made Webley-Fosbery .455 automatic revolver from the spring-retention shoulder holster
with the deftness indicative of much practice, he did not
use it as a firearm. Instead, continuing the swing that
brought it clear, he slammed the six-inch-long hexagonal
barrel against the side of Bradshaw's jaw. Spun around
with his weapon still not clear of leather, the rig being less
suited for rapidity of withdrawal than that of his assailant,
he pitched facedown and unconscious to the ground.

"I saw this yahoo dogging us all the way here," the Texan
commented as he rolled the unresisting enforcer over and
took handcuffs from a pouch at the back of his belt. "So I
figured he might be planning a stickup. Which being, I let
you and Alicia come on down this way to smoke him out
and snuck along the other side of the cars to take him
when he did."

"I'm pleased you did," Wright replied, being so dis-
turbed by the implications of what Bradshaw had said that
he did not notice the girl had behaved in a remarkably
calm way all through the incident. "What're you going to
do?"

"Call a paddy wagon and have him hauled off to the
pokey," the blond giant replied, having handcuffed the unconscious man.

"Do you have to?" the gang leader inquired, his words
stemming from the thought that such a procedure might be
unwise rather than from any sense of loyalty to his enforcer.

"I thought *you'd* want it that way."

"I suppose I *should,* but that would lead to a trial and I'd rather not have the publicity there's sure to be if I have to go to court as a witness."

"Have it your way, Mr. Anstruther," the blond giant assented. "Way you've treated Alicia and me so good, I reckon I owe you that favor. There's one thing, though. You know that stuff you wanted me to find out?"

"Yes," Wright said eagerly.

"Well, I've just about got it all," the Texan announced. "I'll know for sure tomorrow night. Only, I reckon it'll be worth *something*."

"Something?" the gang leader queried and darted a glance at the girl who had drawn back a short distance.

"Oh sure," the blond giant drawled, apparently taking the hint. "This isn't the time and place to talk about it."

"How about my place after we've dropped her off?" Wright suggested, wanting to get an idea of what the information entailed and discuss how much it would cost.

"Not with the way she acts after a night like we've had," the Texan refused with a lecherous grin, looking briefly in the redhead's direction. "It'd be a mortal sin to waste *that*. Anyways, I can't tell you anything until tomorrow evening."

"Very well," the gang leader conceded. "Come around to my place tomor—!"

"Come around, my ass!" the blond giant refused bluntly. "My momma didn't raise no stupid children. I'm not saying there would be, mind, but I don't talk anyplace where there could be folks near to hand listening in to what I say. We'll do the talking where there's no chance of that."

"And where would that be?" Wright inquired, having meant to have the Talker listening in the next room so they would have something incriminating upon which they could blackmail the Texan into complying with future demands instead of requiring payment.

"The house next door's empty," the blond giant answered, gesturing toward the wall surrounding the grounds of the Banyan Club. "You be waiting just inside the front gate at half past eight tomorrow night and I'll drop by to give you everything you want."

"What the hell was Dirty playing at?" Francis Wright demanded in a furious tone. "I know he was hopped up on muggle, but the way he talked, he's blaming me for the boys getting picked up."

"The idea's been getting around," Michael Buffong replied. "It's been noticed that one of the boys gets the arm put on him not long after you've been seen talking to that big blond cop."

"Hell!" the gang leader snapped, staring at the mouthpiece of the telephone. "I've told you why I'm seeing him. He got a traffic ticket squared for me and, even though he hasn't been able to find anything out about the arrests, he went along with me when I said I didn't want Dirty taken in."

"Sure, you told me," the Talker replied, but his voice indicated a lack of conviction. "Now get on to Headquarters and ask for him, then call me back."

After the unconscious enforcer was sent home in a taxi procured by the blond giant, Wright had hardly been able to control his eagerness to contact Buffong. Saying the incident had had an unsteadying effect on his nerves, he had avoided having his guests accompany him to his apartment. On arriving there alone, he had made the telephone call to Buffong. Now, glaring furiously at the instrument as its line went dead, he decided to do what the Talker had demanded, rather than merely suggested before he had hung up on him.

"I'd like to speak to Detective Longley," the gang leader requested, on making the connection he required.

"Who-all're you wanting?" the desk sergeant at the

Headquarters of the Dallas Police Department asked in a Texan's drawl.

"Detective Longley," Wright repeated. "William A. Longley. You'd maybe know him better as 'Bad Bill.' "

"Somebody's been greening you, mister," the desk sergeant declared. "The only Bad Bill Longley I've ever heard tell of was an old-time gunfighter and he got hung back in the 1870s. Who's this calling?"

"All right," the gang leader said, having hung up without supplying the requested information and having contacted Buffong again. "What's it all about?"

"Your 'rotten apple' isn't a detective, as you'll know by now," the Talker replied. "And his name isn't Longley. It's Ranse Smith. He's one of the Counter family and, even though he's worth well over a million bucks, he's a sergeant in the Texas Rangers. What's more, it's *them* and not the local law who've been putting the arm on the boys."

"How long have you known that?"

"I only heard about it tonight, and I'll tell you one thing, Frankie, the boys don't like what's going on!"

"And what is going on?" Wright challenged, despite being able to guess at the conclusions drawn by his men.

"They aren't *sure*," Buffong answered, but his tone implied the opposite. "Only, they reckon no cop like him would need to do favors just for money."

Having long experience of the way gangsters thought, Wright did not take the matter further. Promising he would rectify the situation to the satisfaction of his men on the following evening, he concluded the conversation. Then, sitting slumped in a chair by the telephone, he turned all his attention to thinking over everything that had happened since his first meeting with the blond giant.

Being possessed of considerable intelligence, everything soon became clear to the gang leader. It was obvious that Longley—or Smith—had deliberately set out to make his acquaintance. For some reason, he had failed to do so at the racetrack. However, he had been successful at the North Dallas Golf and Country Club. With the ploy accomplished, including a comment intended to arouse the Talker's suspicions as they were leaving, the arrests of the other members of the gang were timed to coincide with later meetings. Although he had not considered such a possibility earlier, he realized now that—without the fear inspired by their presence—tongues would have started to wag once he and his men had taken their departure. The Philadelphia Police Department must have gathered all the information needed to make the arrests and would have applied to the authorities in Texas for assistance. Clearly the men were being picked up in accordance with a scheme to create suspicion and animosity, rendering them more susceptible to suggestions of betraying the others still at liberty—even himself—in return for personal amnesty.

A sense of fury bit into Wright as he thought of how he had fallen into the trap. It was, he told himself, all the fault of the Talker. If their relationship had continued the way it was while they were in Philadelphia, he would not have succumbed to the temptation to put one over on Buffong. However, he turned his thoughts from taking revenge on his contact man. Before he could do that, he had to reinstate himself with the rest of the gang. He knew there was only one way he could bring them back under his domination. Although it had been some time since he last needed to resort to such measures personally, in earlier years, he had built himself a reputation for being a ruthless killer that eventually elevated him above the rest of the gang and led them to accept him as their leader. Only by showing he was still ready, willing, and able to carry out his own executions could he prove he had not become too soft to maintain his position as boss.

"All right, you smart-assed son of a bitch!" the gang

leader snarled, and all trace of the urbanity he had acquired since his rise to power disappeared. "When you come to see me tomorrow with whatever faked-up news you've got, I'm going to show you the only thing to do with a rotten apple in a barrel."

Standing in the darkness concealed by a stone pillar at the side of the open gate leading to the obviously unoccupied colonial-style mansion next door to the Banyan Club, Francis Wright looked at the luminous dial of his wristwatch. Seeing the time was almost eight twenty-five, he pulled a heavy-caliber Smith & Wesson revolver from his waistband. Although he had done so before leaving his apartment, he checked that its cylinder held six cartridges and was moving smoothly. Then, despite the mechanism being double-action, he set the hammer at fully cocked so as to be able to fire a split second faster when the time came. He had not forgotten how swiftly the blond giant had drawn when striking Dirty Kev Bradshaw down and had no intention of offering an opportunity for it to happen again.

Satisfied with the precautions he had taken, the gang leader leaned forward to peer around the pillar at the generally well lit, but deserted, surrounding area. Just as he was about to withdraw and hide once more, he saw a big black limousine approaching. He expected it to enter one of the other properties that flanked the street, particularly the Banyan Club, but it kept moving until opposite his hiding place. Although the streetlamps were working elsewhere, the one nearest to the gate was out and he was unable to see inside the vehicle. However, he felt sure it must be carrying the man for whom he was waiting.

"Is that you, *Smith*?" the gang leader inquired, keeping the revolver concealed behind his back and stepping forward as the limousine stopped.

"No, you goddamned double-crosser!" replied a voice Wright recognized as belonging to Michael Buffong.

There was no time for the gang leader to realize the mistake he had made. It had been his intention to announce he had learned the young Texan's true identity before opening fire. Instead, he had given the occupants of the limousine what they considered to be the final proof of his perfidy and proposed betrayal.

Already suspecting Wright was planning to get rid of all the gang, then head for somewhere safe with their money, the Talker had received what he regarded as proof that afternoon. He was visited at his apartment by a red-haired and Indian-dark young Texan. Giving the name "Comanche Blood," and saying he knew of the connection between Buffong and Big Frankie Wright, he had announced he had information for sale. Admitting he was there with robbery in mind, he had told how he was at the parking lot of the Banyan Club the previous night and, in addition to seeing what had happened to the enforcer, had overheard the subsequent conversation between the gang leader and Sergeant Ranse Smith of the Texas Rangers. In return for being given twenty-four hours in which to get away, Wright was going to turn over to the blond giant sufficient evidence to ensure the conviction of every member of the gang still at liberty in Dallas. Pressed for further details, in return for all the money Buffong had on the premises, the visitor had disclosed the time and place at which the betrayal was to take place. He had also claimed that Smith had said he was going to handle the whole deal personally and alone so as to be the sole beneficiary of the credit that would accrue from its success.

On being informed of their leader's intentions, the remaining members of the gang were in agreement that he must be prevented from putting the betrayal into effect. They also concurred with the Talker's supposition that

Wright would have all their money somewhere safe so he could pick it up before his flight and, therefore, it was already lost to them. Even if he could be taken alive, when he failed to keep the appointment, Smith would suspect what had happened and would start the hunt for them too quickly for them to be able to induce Wright to tell them where they could collect it.

However, warning them that killing Wright earlier would allow the law to commence searching for them in daylight, the Talker had proposed that it was done just before the rendezvous was to take place. Then, with their revenge achieved, they would have a far better chance of escaping in the darkness. While they all agreed with this plan, he had been less successful with his other proposal. Although he had acquired a foul reputation for his mistreatment of women, albeit unproven as far as the law was concerned, it had always been his policy to avoid personal participation in the gang's various illicit activities. But they were determined that he must become an accessory during the killing, so he could not betray them at some later date, and they had insisted that he accompanied them. Because nobody would agree to anybody else being left behind, they were all in the limousine. However, once the killing was done, they intended to collect other vehicles and scatter.

Even as Michael Buffong replied to Francis Wright, Kevin Bradshaw, holding a Thompson submachine gun despite his face being swathed by bandages supporting his broken jaw, thrust its muzzle through the open rear passenger window and squeezed the trigger. Set for automatic fire, the heavy-caliber weapon chattered harshly in the silence that followed the words. Spreading out like an invisible fan, the .45-caliber bullets engulfed the horrified gang leader. A scream burst from him as several of them tore into his body and flung him backward through the gates. As he went, the Smith & Wesson crashed once to send lead harmlessly into the air before it was released by his lifeless hand.

"Beat it!" the Talker screeched, confident that Wright could not have survived the hail of bullets.

Needing no telling, the man at the steering wheel was already getting ready to set the limousine into motion. However, even as he was starting to release the clutch and operate the accelerator, a truck shot from the next gateway and halted, blocking the street. To provide another source of alarm, a second big vehicle appeared from the entrance to the Banyan Club and behaved in the same fashion. Even if any of the gang had believed their appearance was accidental, the thought would have been dispelled by the spotlights that came on from the back of each truck to illuminate the whole area between them. Furthermore, armed men with the silver five-pointed "star in a circle" badges of the Texas Rangers on their jackets, sprang over the open sides or from the cabs.

"Peace officers here!" boomed a voice clearly augmented by some form of speaking trumpet. "Toss out your guns, then follow them with your hands held high!"

Muttering what would have been "Like hell!" if the words were understandable, Bradshaw kicked open the rear door and thrust himself forward. Knowing he was certain to receive a capital sentence should he be taken alive, he was determined to try to fight his way clear. Alighting on the sidewalk, despite the tommy gun being turned in the other direction, he saw what he decided must be his first target. The blond giant who had broken his jaw the night before at the Banyan Club had leapt from the running board of the second truck and was running forward. Snarling unintelligible profanities, the enforcer started to swing the weapon around to take his revenge.

Riding on the running board as he had been, Sergeant

Ranse Smith was unable to have the weapon he had selected for the operation in his hands. Once again proving
to have had considerable training, the moment his feet
arrived on the ground, he set about rectifying the situation.
Starting to advance, he sent his right hand beneath his
jacket. However, what he brought into view was more potent than the Webley-Fosbery automatic revolver. Carried
in an open-fronted spring-retention holster on a three-
inch-wide belt around his waist, the Burgess Folding Riot
Gun was designed for comparative ease of concealment
combined with speed of operation. Although the barrel
was turned beneath the operating section and butt in the
manner that supplied its name, on being swung forward, it
pivoted on a hinge until it snapped home and automati-
cally locked with the receiver. Such was the excellence of
the design, it was possible to have the tubular magazine
beneath the barrel filled to its six-shot capacity and ready
for use when the weapon was folded for carrying.

Deftly catching the foregrip in his left hand as it rose
and was locked into the operating position, the blond giant
continued to tilt the barrel of the Burgess upward. While
doing this, his right hand was manipulating the longitudi-
nally sliding pistol grip and trigger-guard assembly. This
served the same purpose as the "trombone" type of
foregrip fitted to similar, albeit more conventional, weapons of the same category manufactured by other companies. Having operated the mechanism in a split second, he
saw what Bradshaw was doing and concluded he had been
selected as the next target for some of the bullets left in the
fifty-round drum magazine on the tommy gun. What was
more, he realized there was a problem he must resolve
before he could open fire with his own weapon. The shell
that he had fed into the chamber held a charge of nine
buckshot balls. At the distance they would have to fly, they
would have spread apart to such an extent that those that

missed the enforcer would put in jeopardy the lives of the other members of Company "Z" who were beyond him.

Goaded by a realization that everything was going terribly wrong, the Talker responded with a speed he rarely employed. Shoving open the front passenger door, he dived out of the limousine almost as quickly as Bradshaw. However, it was not his intention to fight. Instead, hoping to escape in the confusion while his companions were resisting, he ran as fast as his legs could carry him across the street toward the open gateway of the mansion at the other side. Seeing Buffong was not holding a weapon of any kind, the oldest of the Texas Rangers snapped an order instead of raising the ancient-looking Winchester Model of 1873 rifle in his hands.

Leaving his master's side in a way far more indicative of the name "Lightning" than was its behavior for much of the time, Sergeant Jubal Branch's big bluetick coonhound sped after the fleeing man. Hearing its pattering feet as he was running along the path toward the mansion, the Talker looked back. Realizing he could not outrun the big dog, he spun around and launched a kick at it. Avoiding the attack, Lightning lunged upward and his powerful jaws closed upon the most vulnerable point of the masculine anatomy. Sudden and nauseating agony ripped through Buffong, and he toppled backward. While doing so, and after he landed on the hard gravel, he struggled, thereby inducing the hold to be continued. By the time pain caused him to lapse into an unconscious state, he was left in no condition to be able to carry out the rape that—frequently accompanied by a brutal beating—had been an all too regular part of his treatment of women in the past, even if he would still have been young enough to follow up such an inclination when he finished the lengthy prison sentence he was to receive.

Skidding to a halt, not for the first time in his comparatively short service as a peace officer, Ranse felt grateful for having acted upon advice given by a more experienced associate. During the preparations for the ambush of the criminals that he had helped to bring about, Sergeant Jubal Branch had suggested how he should load his Burgess. There was, warned the elderly veteran of law enforcement duties for almost as many years as the blond giant had been alive, the chance that the driver of the gang's vehicle might try to crash past the truck blocking the road ahead. If this happened, a charge of buckshot would not be sufficient to stop it. Therefore, although he had a shell with such a load ready to feed into the chamber, the next in the magazine tube was more potent than required just to deal with a man.

While swinging the butt of the riot gun until it was cradled against his right shoulder, Ranse flicked the reloading mechanism back and forward to eject the buckshot and replace it with the next shell. Continuing to move with unflurried speed, despite watching the tommy gun being swung in his direction and being aware of its lethal potential at such close quarters, he squinted along the barrel. Unlike a shotgun used for purely sporting purposes such as hunting flying game birds, the Burgess was equipped with a rudimentary rear and front sight to allow more positive alignment. Completing his aim, even though he could see more members of Company "Z" beyond his objective, he did not hesitate before squeezing the trigger. The gun crashed, but what passed through the barrel was not nine separate balls. Instead, a solid slug .729 of an inch in caliber was sent on its way.

While satisfied that he had held true, the blond giant did not rely upon his summation. Instead, his right hand pulled back and then thrust forward the sliding assembly twice. On the first occasion, the empty case was tossed into the air. However, because the next shell was loaded with buckshot, the second movement ejected and replaced it with its successor, which held another solid ball. Before he had completed the precaution, he saw Bradshaw reel under the impact of the first chunk of lead. Jets of flame burst from the muzzle of the tommy gun, but the barrel had been deflected and the bullets did nothing more than send chips of adobe flying from the surrounding wall of the mansion to the right of the big Texan. The chatter of the deadly weapon ended as the enforcer crumpled backward to go down with a hole in the center of his chest. However, being made of soft lead, the solid ball did not go through his body and endanger the peace officers behind him.

Taking in the sight of the well-armed peace officers who had left the trucks at each end of the limousine, the surviving members of the gang knew resistance would be both futile and almost certainly fatal. First taking the precaution of throwing out their weapons, they yelled that they surrendered and emerged with raised hands as they had been instructed.

"You've got them *all*, Ben," Lieutenant Victorio Bianco enthused, having been brought into town to take part in the ambush.

"Every one," Major Benson Tragg agreed, holding the loudspeaker with which he had delivered the orders. Then he turned his gaze to where one of his men had gone through the gate at which the rendezvous was to take place. "Did they get him?"

"He's cashed in his chips," was the reply.

"Bueno," the commanding officer of Company "Z" declared. "I'd have been real sorry happen this trick we played on good old Big Frankie had wound up with him being taken to hospital—*alive.*"

On hearing that Francis Wright and his gang were in Dallas, being a member of a family whose connections with law enforcement in Texas extended almost as far back as did the Turtles on the other side, Major Benson Tragg had appreciated the danger created by their presence. He knew Hogan Turtle was not acting with the interests of justice at heart when reporting that they had arrived and intended to try to take over the town, but hoped to avert a situation neither of them wanted to arise. Being aware that any attempt to take over would be resisted by Turtle and the other local criminals, he had been determined to prevent gang warfare commencing.

As well as learning all he could about the newcomers from Chief of Police Samuel Ballinger, the Major had had a surveillance of them carried out by his own men. He had also availed himself of the assistance of a friend who was born deaf and, in addition to being able to read lips, was very competent at interpreting what was thought as well as said by studying facial expressions. Watching a meeting between Wright and Michael Buffong, the friend had stated a belief that there was animosity between them and the latter was concerned about a large sum of money belonging to the gang that the former claimed to be in safe-keeping. Using the information he had accrued, Tragg had formulated a plan to deal with the unwanted visitors.

Selected as being the most suitable to play the part, even though it would be his first assignment without the support of a longer-serving companion, Ranse Smith had posed as a dishonest peace officer. To help him with the deception, Rita Yarborough—accepted as an "unofficial official" member of Company "Z"—pretended to be his girlfriend whose extravagant tastes helped to cause him to live beyond his means. Although an attempt to make Wright's acquaintance at the racetrack had failed, there had been an unanticipated bonus. Compelled by circumstances to act without the blond giant's help, "Alicia" had become involved with and brought to justice a trio of criminals engaged in an attempt to swindle the management of the Banyan Club.

Seeking another opportunity to meet the gang leader, Ranse had suggested he put to use his ability as a golfer. What was more, he had arranged this to take advantage of the ill feeling that had developed between Wright and the Talker. To help set the scene, knowing Buffong played every day at the North Dallas Golf and Country Club and had earned a reputation for being a "bandit," Tragg had prevailed upon Judge Jules Robespierre to arrange to meet the gang leader there. Acting the part of a young man with more gullibility and money than skill, the blond giant had persuaded the Talker to challenge him to a round with a good-sized bet at stake. In addition to being a four-handicap player, he possessed a good knowledge of the tricks employed by "bandits" like Buffong and countered them to such good effect that he won a considerable sum of money.

As had been anticipated, having heard about the game and informed that the Judge could not join him, Wright had taken what he considered to be a chance to get to know the young man who had made a sucker out of the Talker. Supplied with the letter from the bank and the "returned" check, the headwaiter had helped to establish that Ranse was a peace officer with financial difficulties and not overburdened by scruples. Once more, the gang leader had reacted as was expected. Wanting to prove himself smarter and more capable than Buffong, he had changed his habit of keeping in the background and had begun to cultivate the "rotten apple in the barrel" he had found.

Wright was correct in his assumption that one of his men had been arrested soon after each of the subsequent meetings with the blond giant that had been witnessed by Kevin Bradshaw. This had caused suspicion among the other members of his gang. On learning that Ranse was wealthy, he had reacted exactly the way it had been hoped he would. He had realized Ranse had no need to accept bribes and presumably was seeking personal aggrandizement for bringing about his downfall, and he had come to the rendezvous they had arranged with revenge by murder in mind. Although it had not been anticipated, the behavior of the enforcer in the parking lot of the Banyan Club had been a worthwhile bonus for having given added credence to another part of the plan. Employing his favorite alias, "Comanche Blood," Sergeant Mark Scrapton had paid the call on Buffong in the guise of a young criminal and had given the information that caused the gang to arrive with the intention of preventing Wright from betraying them.

Although the Philadelphia Police Department had sufficient evidence to convict all the other members of the gang, from the beginning of the operation Major Tragg had known there would be considerable difficulty in making charges against Wright hold up in court. However, the special force of Texas Rangers he commanded had been formed to cope with such situations. Guessing correctly how all of the gang would react, his plan had always been intended to achieve the ending that had, in fact, happened.

Francis "Big Frankie" Wright might have avoided paying the penalty for his numerous crimes if he had been brought to trial.

However, the gang leader had met a well-deserved fate and justice had been done at the hands of Company "Z".

PART FOUR

JESSICA AND TRUDEAU FRONT DE BOEUF

In

THE PENALTY OF FALSE ARREST

"Give me a glass of sarsparilla, please—No, dash it, make that a tall *beer!*"

The man on duty behind the counter noticed the way this particular customer started to give his order, and then changed, using a tone implying a desire to be reckless. This was after he had darted a glance at the front entrance to the Scranton Saloon. The bartender was reminded of a schoolboy checking that he was not under observation by somebody whose authority he feared. Having been a bartender for most of his working life, Harry Trilby considered himself a shrewd judge of character and, business being slack despite the time being half past three on a Saturday afternoon, he studied the speaker with more than just casual interest.

At least six feet two inches in height, the customer was built on massive lines and was in his mid-twenties. Clean shaven, his handsome face was pallid and had an expression of petulance rather than rugged determination. His

voice was just as Trilby expected, having the accent of a
well-bred Southerner and with a soft, mild, almost hesitant
timbre. Despite his exceptional size and bulk, he conveyed
the impression of having received a gentle, even pampered, upbringing somewhere below the Mason-Dixon
line. There was a lethargic air about his movements, and at
first sight, Trilby would not have been surprised if he had
been breathing heavily as the result of taking unaccus-
tomed exercise by walking to the saloon.

While pouring beer from its bottle into a schooner, the
bartender looked more closely at the newcomer. It came as
no surprise that he did not conform with any of the styles
of dress worn by the usual run of visitors—particularly the
railroad workers, cowhands, and buffalo hunters—who
came to Abilene. From beneath a flat check "sporting"
cap, curly mousy brown hair hung somewhat longer than
was regarded as *de rigueur* among cowhands from Texas in
particular; not that anything about him suggested he belonged to that hard-working, hard-fighting, harder-playing
breed. The high collar of his white shirt, which disappeared
into a silver-gray vest without lapels, was embellished by a
neatly fastened black bow tie. Although he did not have
the look of an outdoor man, the rest of his attire was composed of a light-tan-colored yoked shooting jacket, matching knickerbockers, thick woolen argyle plaid stockings,
and well-polished black boots with short gaiters of the kind
known as "spatterdashes." Tidy to the point of being fas-
tidious, the garments had clearly been tailored to his fit.
However, his bearing seemed to imply there was soft flesh
rather than hard muscle under them. What was more, and
the bartender had noticed this early in the examination,
there was nothing to indicate they concealed a weapon of
any kind.

Having been born and raised west of the Mississippi
River, Trilby assessed that the newcomer was not showing

the best of sense by appearing in public dressed in such a fashion, especially on that particular Saturday afternoon. The very capable Town Marshal Stanley Woodrow Markham had already left on a hunting trip for the weekend with the President of the First Stockmen's Bank and a few other cronies. Because of the disinclination of the Mayor and City Council to spend more than was absolutely necessary on paying them, none of his deputies were of such a high quality that they commanded the wholesome respect he had acquired by virtue of his rugged enforcement of the law. Therefore, some of the transient population might decide to take advantage of his absence to "raise a little hell." However, fortunately, there were only a few other customers in the barroom, none of whom would regard the massive young man as an easy target for the baiting or rough horseplay frequently accorded to such an obvious dude by the more rowdy element.

"I'm afraid I don't have anything smaller on me," the newcomer said on being told what he owed for the beer that was placed in front of him, bringing a thick bundle of money from inside his jacket and peeling away a ten-dollar bill. "And please take a drink for yourself out of it."

"Thank you, sir," Trilby replied, then noticed the appearance of the money was attracting the attention of three men sitting at a nearby table.

Always on the alert to pick out potential trouble-causers, the bartender had scrutinized the trio when they came in shortly after he opened up. From their Eastern style of clothing and snatches of conversation that reached his ears, he had concluded they were traveling salesmen of some kind. If that was the case, they had not shown any signs of being in a hurry to go about their business. Instead, they had sat making a couple of beers apiece last a considerable time and, while playing an apparently cheerful and noisy game of poker with a deck of cards borrowed from him, had looked over everybody else who came in. Watching and listening, he had ascertained that—in the order of their respective size—they answered to the names "Sheets," "Dishpan," and what sounded like "Un-Mench."

After having exchanged glances and nods of what appeared to be confirmation with his companions, "Sheets" picked up their glasses and, shoving back his chair, he rose to walk across the room. Despite the bar being empty along the rest of its length, he made his way straight toward where the massive newcomer was standing. Arriving, he contrived to jog the young man's elbow. Concluding this was not accidental, Trilby wondered why he was behaving in such a fashion. While the tallest and most heavily built of the trio, he could not match the newcomer in size and heft. Nor, particularly as he had imbibed only two beers since entering and had seemed completely sober when ordering the first, did he have the look of one who had drunk sufficient hard liquor to be "on the prod" and seeking to impress his companions by picking a fight with a bigger opponent. Another possibility came to the bartender's mind, but he decided to see how the situation developed before taking any action.

"Sorry, friend," Sheets said, as some of the beer held by the newcomer was spilled. His heavily mustached broad face had lines suggesting a jolly nature, but there was a hard and calculating glint to his eyes. "Here, let me have your schooner filled up again."

"No, thank you, sir," the young man replied, his voice redolent of politeness rather than annoyance. "It was an accident."

"Sure, that's all it was," Sheets confirmed. "But I'd feel a whole heap better was you to let me buy you one for what I've spilled."

"Oh very well," the young man acceded, after another seemingly worried glance at the batwing doors of the front entrance. "As it's your health that's at stake, I'll agree with pleasure."

"My *health*?" Sheets queried, looking blank for a moment. Then understanding came and, letting out a booming guffaw of laughter, he slapped his right hand against his thigh. "Hey, that's a *good* one. Damn me, I'll have to remember to use it the first time I get the chance."

"If you thought that one was good," the young man drawled, clearly delighted by the response to his remark. "Do you know why the chicken crossed the road?"

"No," Sheets replied, with such apparent sincerity he might have been speaking the truth. "Why did the chicken cross the road?"

"For some foul reason," the young man supplied.

"By golly, if you aren't a *card*!" Sheets bellowed, after mirth far in excess of what the feeble and very old joke warranted to the bartender's way of thinking. "Hey, I bet you know a whole heap more like that. Seeing's how you're on your lonesome, why don't you come over and join us. The boys'll really enjoy hearing 'em."

"That's most kind of you, sir," the young man declared. "Time was hanging rather heavily on my hands with moth— Yes, I'd admire to join you."

Watching the newcomer accompanying Sheets to the table and sitting down, Trilby frowned. Except that he did not believe the trio to be professional gamblers, he could see a pattern emerging with which he was all too familiar. However, the supposition he formed placed him on the horns of a dilemma. Although he was expected to divert trouble, if possible before it could start, there were limits to how far he could go without provoking it himself. He could not intervene in the present situation merely on the strength of what he believed might be planned, and it would be sure to create resentment, even complaints to his employer, should his suspicions be unjustified. Deciding he would keep the group under observation, he turned his attention to a customer who had come to the bar and was waiting impatiently to be served.

"Hey, fellers," Sheets said. Pausing and glancing in an interrogatory fashion at the guest he had brought to the table, he continued, "This here's Mr.—"

"The name is Trudeau Front de Boeuf, gentlemen, from Beaufort Parrish, Louisiana," the young man responded to what had clearly been a request for such information. "But my friends call me 'Beef-Head.' That's my name translated from French into English, you know."

"Glad to meet you, Beef-Head," the tallest of the trio boomed, extending his big right hand to be enfolded in an even larger white palm that was smoothly soft to the touch and seemed incapable of exerting any strength. "I'm Harvey Q. Forrest, but they call me 'Sheets' 'cause I travel in bed linen."

"You're wearing clothes like the rest of us today," Front de Boeuf remarked, with the air of believing he was making an original and most witty comment.

"By cracky, boys, is he a card or is he a *card*?" Sheets boomed, and his companions contrived to appear equally amused by the feeble attempt at humor. "This here's Un-Mench. It's short for 'Un-mentionables,' and we call him that 'cause he's a drummer for them fancy doodads we all know's ladies wear under their dresses. And this's Dishpan. He sells kitchenware."

"I'm pleased to make your acquaintance, gentlemen," Front de Boeuf asserted, then glanced at the cards and money on the table. "But aren't I interrupting your game?"

"Well, yes, I reckon you might say that," Sheets admitted. "But I reckon the boys would rather hear some of your jokes."

"I would," asserted Un-Mench. Surly looking, he was of

medium height, with a bulky frame that had run to fat. "I can always use some new 'n's."

"Trust you pair to want to quit," Dishpan growled. Being almost as tall as the bed linen salesman albeit much slimmer, he had a sallow, foxy cast of features. "No offense, Beef-Head, but they're doing all the winning and I'd sure like a chance to get my money back."

"I can understand that," Front de Boeuf declared, but he was not entirely successful in trying to convey the impression that he was an experienced man of the world. "I always like to win it back when I'm gambling and losing."

"Don't tell me *you* play poker?" Sheets inquired.

"I haven't played recently, mother doesn—" Front de Boeuf replied, then cut off his words abruptly and looked sheepish, as if realizing he was making a less than manly statement. Avoiding the eyes of the three drummers, he went on, "Not since I left college, but I was known as being quite a poker-wolf while I was there."

"I just bet you were," Un-Mench said. "Fact being, I'd say you was a mite too good for the likes of us. We only play for the fun of it."

"So do I, sir," the massive young man protested. "Land's sakes, you don't think I'm a *card-sharper,* do you?"

"Of course we don't," Sheets answered reassuringly. "It's just old Un-Mench's way of joshing you."

"Yeah," seconded the salesman of ladies' underclothing. "No offense meant, Beef-Head."

"None taken, then," Front de Boeuf declared, looking mollified.

"I'm pleased to hear it," Un-Mench asserted. "Say, happen you've a mind, I'll show you some of the fancy doodads I'm peddling."

"Later, perhaps," the massive young man replied, but without showing any great enthusiasm for the opportunity to view female "unmentionables." "Right now, I'd rather play some poker."

"Then let's get to playing some," Sheets suggested, reaching for the deck and holding it toward his guest. "Here, you have first deal."

"How about *these*, Mrs. Front de Boeuf?" inquired Cuthbert Alan Bleasdale the Third, waving a hand at the animals crowded into the two corrals behind his livery barn. Only just five feet seven in height and corpulent, there was an expression suggestive of a desire to be helpful on his less than prepossessing florid face. As usual, he was clad in an expensive, somber-colored, and somewhat old-fashioned style calculated to inspire confidence in his integrity. His appearance and the sober, upright, piously churchgoing members of the community with whom he associated were assets in his business as a horse trader. "I think you'll agree that they're just what you're after."

"I'm not so sure," replied the woman to whom the comment was addressed. In comparison with the somewhat nasal Midwest accent of the man by her side, her rich contralto voice had the timbre of a well-educated and imperious Southron long accustomed to having her every whim gratified. "They aren't very *big*."

In any kind of company, Jessica Front de Boeuf would have been an imposing figure. Five feet nine in height and in her early forties, she had on a Wavelean straw hat with a spray of guinea fowl plumes at the front, secured by a decorative pin to elegantly piled up black hair, which made her appear to tower over Bleasdale. Although the texture of her skin was beginning to coarsen a trifle more than could be hidden by the amount of makeup permissible for a "good woman," and despite being somewhat marred by lines indicative of an arrogant and domineering nature, her olive-skinned face was beautiful. Obviously selected to take advantage of the current style in acceptable feminine attire and yet seeking successfully to avoid offending the susceptibilities of the kind of people with whom she was mingling in Abilene, her obviously expensive brown two-piece traveling suit and royal-blue silk blouse emphasized the curvaceous fullness of her Junoesque figure's "hour-glass" contours. The jewelry that glistened on her wrists and fingers and about her throat appeared to be equally tasteful and costly. Despite the weather being mild, she had a brown fur muff on her left hand and the right grasped the carrying strap of a neat matching leather reti-cule.

"Well, no, they aren't very big," Bleasdale conceded. "They weren't bred for *size,* but every one of them is up to carrying a goodly weight over rough country and has *proved* it. Don't forget they've been ridden all the way from Southern Texas and worked hard while carrying a man—and we both know how big those Texans can be—as well as all his gear and one of those *massive* saddles they use. They're bred for stamina and to be fast on their feet. Just what the deer-hunting gentlemen down in Louisiana who'll be your customers need, in fact."

"That's the kind of mounts they need, I must admit," Jessica answered, but she did not sound entirely convinced.

"Then these are the ones for you," Bleasdale asserted. "You won't be offered another bunch like this in the whole of Kansas, ma'am."

Which anybody with a greater knowledge of horses than the prospective customer appeared to possess, would have said was probably quite true, unless one's luck was really bad.

Such a person might also have added that no valid rea-son existed why there should be "another bunch like this".

Bleasdale had spoken the truth when claiming the ma-jority of horses used by the Texans bringing herds of half-wild longhorn cattle to the railroad towns in Kansas possessed the qualities he described. What was more, despite their comparatively small size, they would be ideally suited for following hounds that were chasing deer over rough terrain when well bred and in peak condition. However, not one of the animals in the corral would measure up to such a high standard. They were, in fact, the culls sold off as being worthless as working mounts—or having undesirable traits such as "bunch quitting," breaking away from the *remuda* and "heading for parts unknown"—by various trail bosses who didn't want the trouble involved in taking them home. He had obtained them cheaply and, until hearing of the scheme that brought the Southron woman to Abilene, had been meaning to pass them on to a purchaser employed by the United States Cavalry and who was as lacking in scruples as himself. Hoping to obtain a much better price, he had made the acquaintance of Mrs. Jessica Front de Boeuf and, "learning" of her purpose during their first conversation, had offered to help her make the purchases she required.

"You're *sure* they're all right?" Jessica inquired.

"I give you my *word* on it," Bleasdale replied, disregarding the fact that there were animals in the corrals that possessed every possible fault they could while still remaining on their feet. "Of course, if you wish you can have our local veterinarian examine them— Oh *blast* it, if you'll forgive me for using such a term in your presence."

"What's wrong?" Jessica asked, the last comment having been delivered in tones of exasperation.

"He's gone hunting with the Marshal and some other friends and won't be back until late tomorrow night."

"I could wait until Monday and have him look them over," Jessica remarked pensively.

"That you could," Bleasdale agreed, employing what sounded like enthusiasm, although such an examination—

especially when carried out by a man who suffered from no delusions about his true character and would not be afraid to tell the truth—was the last thing he would wish to take place. "Except—"

"Except?" the Southron woman prompted.

"Well, Mr. Titus Merridew, the horse buyer for the U.S. Cavalry, is in town," Bleasdale explained, which was true, as the man in question had arrived on the noon train. However, what he said next did not have a similar veracity. "He's got his eye on this bunch and he's had the veterinarian satisfy him that they are what he needs."

"Has he now?" Jessica asked, looking perturbed. "Would you mind telling me how much he's offered for them?"

"Seventeen hundred and fifty dollars."

"Hmm! Will he go as high as two thousand?"

"Yes."

"How about *two thousand five hundred*?"

"No," the horse trader admitted, his instincts telling him the woman would not increase the price.

"Then, sir," Jessica said in determined tones. "Unless you have any objections to selling them to me instead of the Yank—*U.S.* Cavalry, that is my offer for them."

"A good businessman always takes the *best* deal he's offered," Bleasdale claimed. "So, Mrs. Front de Boeuf, you've got yourself a deal and a *bargain*."

"I have, providing you will throw in their keep until I can have them moved out on Monday's eastbound train," Jessica corrected. "My poppa always told me there should be some 'boot' to every trading deal."

"And he was right," the horse trader affirmed, being so pleased to sell the entire bunch at such a substantial profit —far above the best he could have expected from Titus Merridew, or any other source available elsewhere—that he was willing to forgo the small sum feeding them would cost.

"I don't carry around so much cash money, especially when I'm in Yank—," Jessica began, but halted just in time from making what she apparently realized could prove an offensive remark that might even spoil the deal she had just concluded. Opening her reticule, she continued, "But I'll give you a draft against the First Stockmen's Bank to cover the sum."

For a moment, Bleasdale did not speak. Eager as he was to complete the lucrative deal, he remembered that the president of the bank had left on the hunting trip with the marshal and, when indulging in such a pastime, he invariably closed the premises prior to his departure on the grounds that the staff should not be expected to work if he was off enjoying himself. However, a moment's thought reassured the horse trader that the method of payment would prove satisfactory. The train upon which his victim intended to transport her purchase did not leave until shortly after noon on Monday, and he would have cashed the draft as soon as the bank opened in the morning.

"That will suit me just fine," Bleasdale declared, accepting the proffered bank draft. "So I'll go into the office and fetch you a bill of sale—" Seeing the woman showing signs of accompanying him, he went on hurriedly, "I'd wait here, if I was you, Mrs. Front de Boeuf. While you won't find a *cleaner* place anywhere, a lady of your quality might still find the smell somewhat overpowering."

"As you will," Jessica acceded. "And may I say it's *very* refreshing to receive such consideration from a Yankee."

If the woman had seen the scowl that came to Bleasdale's face as he turned away, she would have known she had been correct in refraining from referring to "Yankee country" earlier in their conversation. The frown had not disappeared when he entered the big main building. There was the real reason he had been disinclined to let her accompany him. The two men who slouched from his office at the rear wore the dress style of cowhands, but nobody who knew the West would have believed this was their real vocation. Tall, lanky, uncleanly, and stubble-featured, the guns in their tied-down holsters gave an indication of the means by which they earned their living. Even if the woman lacked the knowledge to draw the appropriate conclusion, they were sufficiently unprepossessing in appearance to have aroused suspicion when she saw them emerging from the room in which he conducted much of his business and had the words "PRIVATE, No Admittance" inscribed on its door.

"How soon do you want them hosses fetching in from your place?" asked the taller of the pair, who was currently calling himself "Dick Lester."

"You can bring them as far as the woodland north of town on Monday afternoon," Bleasdale replied. "But don't fetch them in here until after sundown."

"Hell, all their brands've been vented until nobody can say who owned 'em," protested the other man, whose "summer name" was supplied as being "Tom Clarke" despite having a strong family resemblance to Lester.

"You came by them *honestly* as far as I know," Bleasdale growled, despite being aware that the ownership of the animals under discussion was questionable to say the least. "And that's not why I don't want them here earlier. I won't be getting the corrals emptied before then."

"You mean you've found a sucker to take that bunch of worthless crowbait?" Lester asked, his harsh Illinois accent expressing incredulity.

"I've sold the whole herd *legitimately* to a customer," the horse trader corrected pompously. Despite his belief that he was quite safe in accepting the offered bank draft, it was not in his nature to take chances and he went on, "So I want one of you to keep an eye on her until Monday for me. If she tries to move them out before it's time for the eastbound train, let me know straightaway."

"Er—just one thing before we start," Trudeau Front de Boeuf said, instead of accepting the deck of cards being offered to him by the tallest of the three drummers. "Are we playing table stakes—I think the word is?"

"Table stakes?" Sheets growled and something of his true nature showed for a moment.

"That is how we always used to play in college," the massive young man explained. "The fellers said they weren't going to take a chance on me—*anybody* signing IOU's or bank drafts moth—that wouldn't be honored when they were presented."

"This here's only a *friendly* game," Sheets asserted, although guessing the precaution was taken because the other players knew Front de Boeuf's mother—who appeared to exert considerable control over him, if his behavior and comments were any guide—would refuse to settle any gambling debts.

"And making it table stakes'll keep it friendly," Un-Mench put in, duplicating the summations. Taking out all the money he had in his possession, he slapped it onto the table and continued, "So let's do just that."

"I'm for it," Dishpan seconded, also producing and putting down his money.

"I'll go with the rest of you," Sheets supported, contriving to sound satisfied with the arrangement. In spite of this, knowing the less than healthy state of his and the other two's finances, he was aware of the disadvantage that might arise through playing for table stakes. Even added together, their money did not equal the amount in the bankroll that the massive young man brought out. However, he decided this was a minor matter and they would be content with that sum instead of obtaining promissory notes that would not be honored. "Let's get started."

Despite his claim to be a most experienced poker player, the way in which Front de Boeuf handled the deck he accepted was far from impressive. After dropping and gathering up several cards in the course of the clumsy overhand shuffle he performed, he placed the deck in front of Un-Mench to be cut. Then, as he was retrieving it, he glanced at the front entrance with such a worried expression it caused the other three to follow his example. They could see nothing to account for his behavior, and by the time they returned their eyes to the table, he had commenced dealing with no greater display of skill.

After hesitantly joining the opening round of betting, when it came to his turn, Front de Boeuf drew two cards. Studying the three aces he had received on the deal and did not improve upon, Sheets gave a slight shake of his head that stopped his companions from staying in and possibly frightening the young man into dropping out of the pot. He knew his hand would beat whichever of the "three of a kinds" he suspected was held by Front de Boeuf, unless the two cards drawn increased them to a full house or four of a kind. Watching how the young man reacted and basing his assumption on what he had already seen, he felt sure this had not happened. For one thing, he believed there would have been some show of elation from the recipient if the draw had produced either a pair or the fourth card to create a much more powerful hand. Failing to detect any, his summations gained what he considered verification when his bet was raised only by a small sum rather than the sizable amount he did not doubt would have resulted from a better hand.

"I'll call," Sheets said, not wanting to drive the young man from the game by making too large a win on the first pot.

"A high straight, I think it's called," Front de Boeuf replied with a self-satisfied smirk, turning his cards over to show the king of hearts, queen of spades, jack of diamonds, and ten and nine of clubs.

"That's a high straight, all right," the tallest drummer growled, but brightened up as he thought of how much easier it would be to win from a man who drew two cards to fill a straight. Such was hardly the act of one who claimed to be a "poker wolf," even if the term was only awarded at some college. However, having achieved the sought-after improvement—despite the odds against success being so high no player of experience would chance it —he was likely to continue to make such a generally ill-advised draw. "You win."

Gathering up the money, Front de Boeuf sorted it out and placed it fastidiously on the thick pile he had transferred from his inside breast pocket to the table in front of him. While he was doing so, Dishpan riffled the deck for the next pot. As the game continued, none of the players realized they were being watched intermittently by a pair of shrewd and discerning eyes.

As he had promised himself, Harry Trilby kept the game under observation when he had nothing else demanding his attention. Before long, he concluded his summations regarding the drummers were correct. None of them showed any signs of employing the skills at cheating that were part of the stock in trade of some professional gamblers with whom he was acquainted, and he decided they were playing a comparatively honest game. However, their attempts at combining their betting to "sandbag" Front de Boeuf into going higher than he would have wished, or to make him fold a potentially winning hand, repeatedly failed to meet with any success. Either by shrewd judgment or pure luck—which seemed more likely when taken into consideration with the rest of his play—he avoided being trapped. What was more, it was soon obvious that he was winning steadily instead of being taken for his bankroll, as the bartender still believed had been the original intention of his opponents.

"By cracky!" Front de Boeuf boomed, exuding a winner's joviality, as he drew in another pot. "What a pleasant way to spend an afternoon."

"Yeah," Sheets replied, but neither he nor the other two drummers looked anywhere near so enthusiastic.

Trilby had been correct with regard to the trio's motives for getting the massive young man into the game and also correct in his estimation of their abilities. While unscrupulous enough to want to take advantage of him, none of them possessed sufficient of the manipulative skills necessary to do so. Instead, having traveled as a group for a couple of years while selling their respective wares, it was their intention to employ tactics that had proved successful in other places.

Unfortunately for the drummers, as they had realized from the beginning might prove the case, the insistence of their intended victim on having table stakes placed them at a serious disadvantage. Although there was nothing in his tactics to suggest he had played anything other than infrequently, he had far more money than they possessed. Therefore, when he held what they guessed from his behavior must be a powerful hand, he was able to avoid being driven out by the sandbag tactics that proved so efficacious elsewhere. In fact, his luck had remained so consistently good that their finances were decreasing to an alarming extent. Exchanging glances with his companions, Sheets concluded they were in agreement with him that the situation must be rectified by a means that had produced a change in their fortunes on several other occasions.

"Damn it!" Dishpan swore, contriving to knock over the schooner of beer that Front de Boeuf had insisted on buy-

ing after winning a large pot instead of being sandbagged
out of it. Watching the liquid flow over the cards, he went
on with a similar exasperation, "We can't keep on using
these!"

"I'll take 'em to the bartender and get another deck,"
Sheets offered and acted upon the suggestion before anybody else could speak.

Explaining to Trilby that there had been an accident, the
tallest drummer was given a fresh deck with a request that
greater care should be taken with it. Agreeing to the stipu-
lation, he turned away from the counter. He was pleased
that business had improved while the game was taking
place so that the bartender was compelled to turn to another customer almost immediately. What was more, as he
had anticipated, his companions were keeping Front de
Boeuf's attention occupied. Dropping the cards—which
were a brand very common throughout the country—into
the left side pocket of his jacket, he removed what appeared to be an identical deck from the right. A wolfish
grin came to his face as he made the switch, then returned
to the table prepared to lead their lamb to the slaughter.

"Mr. Merridew?"

"That's me, ma'am," replied the man to whom Jessica
Front de Boeuf had spoken.

"I understand you're the buyer of horses for the Yank—
U.S. Cavalry?"

"For the Army as a whole, ma'am. I buy them for draft
purposes as well as riding."

Although the first part of his surname was reflected in
his looks, people who knew Titus Merridew well considered he was a perfect example of just how deceptive looks
could be. Built on large lines—although obviously having
allowed himself to run to fat—he had a sun-reddened face
that implied the jovially convivial nature of one wanting

only to be helpful to others. In fact, it and his general demeanor suggested he was a man to be trusted under any and every circumstance. He invariably dressed neatly, but not so expensively as to arouse suspicions about the possibility of sources of income other than his official salary. Instead, he sought and, indeed, contrived to convey the impression of spending his own hard-earned money on his appearance so as to uphold the dignity of his responsible position.

"I hope you don't object to me seeking you out here to talk business," Jessica said, glancing around the lobby of the Railroad Hotel.

"Certainly not, ma'am," Merridew replied and, as it tended to serve as an implication of his honesty and devotion to duty, he went on with his usual explanation for taking accommodation at the best hotel in town. "My expenses don't cover staying here, but I feel it is incumbent upon my position to do so and I *never* object to talking business wherever I find myself. Shall we go and sit in one of the alcoves while we talk?"

"That's most considerate of you, sir," Jessica declared.

"Now, ma'am," Merridew said after they had seated themselves. "What can I do for you?"

"I have recently bought a number of horses for a scheme I had become interested in at home in Beaufort Parrish, Louisiana," Jessica explained. "Unfortunately, I have just received notification from my principals that the deal is off."

"That's hard luck," sympathized the bulky horse-buyer. Having a discerning eye for the opposite sex, he decided his companion was a very fine-looking woman, even though no longer in the first flush of youth, and it might prove beneficial if he could be of assistance to her. "How can I help you?"

"I was hoping you might consider taking them off my

hands," Jessica answered. "After all, you are here to buy horses for the Cavalry—the Army as a whole—aren't you?"

"That's why I'm here," Merridew confirmed. "And I'll be willing to look your horses over. Where are they?"

"In the corrals behind Bleasdale's Livery Barn," Jessica replied.

"Bleasdale's?" the horse buyer exclaimed before he could stop himself, but long experience acquired at his trade allowed him to control his surprise after the word. "Do you mean they belong to you?"

"I do and I have a bill of sale to prove it," the woman confirmed, reaching into the mouth of her reticule and producing the document. "Mr. Bleasdale sold them to me and assured me they would be ideal for my purpose."

The latter piece of information did not come as any surprise to Merridew as he took the bill of sale. Over the years, he had had sufficient contact with Bleasdale to have no illusions where the other's business scruples were concerned. What was more, as was his invariable habit, he had visited the livery barn without its owner's knowledge shortly after arriving in town and had formed a very accurate estimation of the quality of animals he would be offered when he paid his official call on Monday. That somebody else would have already purchased them had never entered his head. If it had, he would have dismissed it as beyond the realms of possibility.

"You can count on Mr. Bleasdale for *that*," the horse buyer said enigmatically. "So you want to sell the horses, huh?"

"I certainly do," Jessica agreed. "They're no longer of any use to me, and I want to leave for the East tomorrow morning. Can you help me?"

"Well, ma'am, I'd admire to," Merridew declared, her last sentence having been spoken in a manner that implied there would be considerable gratitude involved if she received an affirmative answer. "It all depends upon how much you want for them. You see, I've already seen them and, to tell you the truth, they aren't worth very much."

"You mean Mr. Bleasdale *tricked* me?" Jessica asked indignantly.

"I wouldn't want to go so far as to say *that*," Merridew answered tactfully. "But he has been known to charge too high a price. Not as out-and-out trickery, mind, but as a matter of business."

"How much would *you* be willing to offer me for them?" Jessica inquired, looking at him in a fashion that aroused the horse buyer's willingness to be helpful provided it would not involved him in too great an expenditure of cash.

"Well, as I said, they aren't very good animals. In fact, they're a pretty poor lot. I don't think I could go beyond five hundred dollars for the whole bunch."

"Five hundred?"

"It's not much, I'll grant you. But I'm accountable to the Quartermaster General in Washington, and the prices he allows me to pay aren't munificent."

"But only *five hundred*," Jessica groaned, looking pathetic and distraught. "Why, that will barely cover the money I've spent coming here, much less going home. I did *so* hope for a better sum."

"Well, I suppose I could go as high as seven hundred and fifty," Merridew hinted.

"You couldn't make it a thousand, by any chance?" Jessica suggested. "I would be *so* grateful if you could."

"Damn it, ma'am," Merridew replied, reading an invitation that could offer a satisfying—albeit not monetary— addition to the profit he could still expect at the stipulated price if he agreed. "A thousand it is, and I'll take the loss from my commission."

"Good heavens, sir," Jessica gasped. "I couldn't ask you to do *that*."

"I'd consider it a privilege, ma'am," the horse buyer declared. "Just as I would be honored if you'd be my guest for dinner tonight."

"Why, that would be my pleasure, sir," Jessica affirmed. "There is one *little* thing, though."

"What would that be, ma'am?" Merridew asked, hoping the answer would not be the inclusion of a chaperone at the meal.

"I have some bills to settle and insufficient money to do so," Jessica explained. "And, as the bank won't be open until Monday and I have to leave in the morning, I hope you can pay me in cash."

"Certainly I can," the horse buyer confirmed, having examined the bill of sale—from which Bleasdale had excluded the sum of money involved—during the conversation and satisfied himself it was genuine. "I can get it from the hotel safe and pay you now."

"I'm getting tired of playing poker," Un-Mench was saying as Sheets arrived at the table. "Let's make a change, shall we?"

"Sure," Dishpan supported. "Hey, how about us trying a game I saw being played in Kansas City last fall?"

"What would that be?" Trudeau Front de Boeuf inquired, instead of protesting against the suggestion to change from a game at which he had done very well.

"It's called 'banker and broker,' 'cording to the jaspers who showed me how to play," Dishpan replied, but he was not allowed to continue.

"I don't go a whole heap on putting money on a game I've never even heard of," Un-Mench protested, as he had done on other occasions when it was necessary to help lull any suspicions an intended victim might nourish.

"Hell, it's so simple even *you* could get to know how to play real *easy*," Dishpan countered. "You don't even have to worry about the suits, only the number of the cards. We cut for who holds the bank. After the rest of us take a cut apiece, we show what we've got on the bottom and say how much we want to bet. Then the banker cuts. If he gets lower'n you, he loses. If he cuts higher, he wins. You keep the bank until somebody beats your card, then he gets it until he gets beat hisself. And that's all there is to it. Mind you, it's a game for real *sports*."

"It sounds like it could be fun," the massive young man claimed. "In fact, I've played it before, but under a different name. There's one thing, though. The way we played in college, if you tie with the banker on your cut, there is a standoff, no money changes hands, and you both cut again for a decision."

"That's how I've seen it played," Sheets lied. Usually the banker was the winner in the event of the value of the card he exposed equaling that of a player. However, with the deck he had substituted while returning from the bar, any advantage that might have accrued from a "standoff"— with no payment being made in either direction and another cut taking place to settle the issue—was completely nullified. "What say we give it a whirl?"

"I dunno," mumbled the salesman for ladies' underwear, as was required, when Front de Boeuf did not comment further upon the rules propounded by Dishpan.

"Huh!" The kitchenware salesman snorted derisively, concluding that the victim accepted any changes in the rules from the last time he had played banker and broker as resulting from local variations rather than being—as was the case—to allow the modifications made to the deck to operate against him. "You never was much of a sport, Un-Mench. How's about it, Beef-Head, are you game enough to play."

"I most certainly *am*," Front de Boeuf declared, confirming the supposition of the trio that he would wish to prove himself to be a "sport," willing to join in any kind of game if it achieved this end.

"And me," Sheets seconded.

"Aw hell!" Un-Mench grunted, giving a shrug. "I'll go along with the rest of you."

"Here's the *new* deck from the bar, then," Sheets announced, sitting down and starting to rifle the cards. "Let's get to it."

Satisfied that they at last had the victim where they wanted him, the trio allowed him to make the first cut. The cards for Sheets and Dishpan were lower in value than the eight of hearts he produced, but it was beaten by the king of spades Un-Mench turned up. As the salesmen had hoped would prove the case, Front de Boeuf attached no significance to the difference in the way the final cut was made. Whereas the other two losers and their intended victim did so in the usual fashion, by taking hold of the long side of the deck, Un-Mench's forefinger and thumb closed upon the narrower ends. Despite this appearing to be a harmless idiosyncrasy, it changed banker and broker from a game of chance into a highly efficacious cheating proposition.

Known as "humps," or "belly strippers," the deck of cards in use had been prepared to practically alleviate chance for those conversant with their secret when a cut was carried out. Having been obtained from a legitimate source and as issued by the manufacturer, a dishonest dealer in gambling equipment had altered them so as to ensure either an ace or a king could be cut at will by his customer. To ensure this, the other forty-four cards had been shortened by a thirty-secondth of an inch on the narrow end and their corners rounded again. Next, the required aces and kings were treated so they had a slight "belly" that protruded at the middle of each narrow end. Unless a much closer examination was carried out than the trio intended to permit, the result was barely discernible to the naked eye. Nevertheless, to one who knew the secret of their operation, they were invaluable in the version of banker and broker being played. What was more, as Sheets had appreciated when purchasing the deck, they did not require the long training necessary to develop the manipulative skills that were essential for more subtle methods of cheating.

"What'll you bet, Beef-Head?" Un-Mench inquired after his companions had shown their selections and, also by cutting in the conventional fashion, the young man had exposed a queen. Having acquired low cards, Sheets and Dishpan had already only put up a couple of dollars apiece. "Are you going to be a *piker* like them?"

"Mine's worth ten dollars," Front de Boeuf declared, the comment about the small wagers made by the other two having produced the required response. "No, dash it, make that *twenty*. Unless you want to set a limit, that is."

"No limits for *me*. I'm no piker like some not too far away," Un-Mench confirmed. Making the declaration, he cut as he had to win the bank. Finding the humps without difficulty, he raised the segment to show an ace on the bottom and a timbre of spurious sympathy came into his voice. "Now isn't that hard luck for you. I've licked you all."

"You win some and you lose some," Sheets answered, with an equally false air of philosophical acceptance. "Let's give her another whirl."

The game continued and, being in contention against the manipulation of the "humps," Front de Bouef enjoyed none of the success that had favored him while playing poker. Although the trio were too smart to make him the loser every time, even some of the occasional conventional cuts by whichever of them was holding the bank went against him. Therefore, one way or another, he lost all of his previous winnings and some of his original table stake. At last, however, a turn at fair cutting gave him the highest card and with it the advantage of becoming banker.

"Good heavens, is *that* the time?" the young man exclaimed, looking at the clock on the wall behind the bar. "I can't stay much longer, moth— I have an appointment I must keep."

"We'll call it quits," Sheets offered, albeit looking with avarice at the money that still remained in front of the intended victim. "Happen that's how it has to be for you."

"Sure," Un-Mench went on. "It wouldn't do for you to keep your *mother* waiting."

"I can manage a few more hands," Front de Boeuf declared, responding in the manner that the remarks—especially the reference to his mother—were intended to provoke. "Let's make it worthwhile, shall we?"

"How'd you mean?" Dishpan queried and the other two showed a similar interest.

"Let's make it a hundred dollars a cut," Front de Boeuf suggested.

"I'm game if you boys are," Sheets asserted, and even though the sum would require almost all of the money each had before him, his companions registered a similar acquiescence.

Having finally noticed that the bartender was watching them when his duties permitted, the trio glanced his way. Discovering he was currently keeping them under observation and suspecting he would know what they were up to, they decided against employing the type of cut that utilized the modifications to the deck. Nor did it strike them that there was any necessity to do so. The odds were three to one in their favor, and even without all of them beating whatever card was cut by Front de Boeuf, even a single success would add to their combined winnings. What was more, should he be only moderately fortunate, their victim would be made more susceptible to suggestions that he carry on.

"Seven," Sheets announced, showing his card.

"Eight," Un-Mench went on, sounding even more pleased.

"*Queen!*" Dishpan enthused, knowing—as the game was being played—a standoff was the best result available to the intended victim and he would have a second chance to produce a winning number.

"Then here I go," Front de Boeuf said almost mildly.

Although he had cut the deck in the conventional manner until that moment, the massive young man did not on this occasion. Instead, he reached forward with his big hand to take hold of the narrow ends with the tips of his right thumb and forefinger. What was more, his grip proved sufficiently delicate to catch one of the humps.

"Will you just look at *that*—it's a *king!*" Front de Bouef said in tones of delight as he raised his hand to display the bottom card of the pile he was holding. Then, moving more swiftly than at any other time since the gambling had commenced, he dropped the cards and gathered up the money that had been wagered to place it on the pile in front of him. Thrusting the now sizable stack into the breast pocket from which his table stakes had come, he went on, "I'm sorry, gentlemen, but I *must* pull out *now*."

"Hold hard there!" Sheets spat out furiously, seeing the attention of the bartender had been distracted by a customer. "What's the game?"

"*Game?*" Front de Boeuf repeated, looking puzzled. "I thought you said it was called banker and broker."

"Don't get smart-assed with me!" the largest of the salesmen snarled, and his companions exuded a similar menace. "Why'd you make that goddamned cut the way you did?"

"Well," the massive young man answered, his manner still mild. "I'd seen all of you do it that way, and when you did, you were *always* lucky. So I thought I would see if worked for me—And it *did*."

"Don't try to feed us that crap!" Sheets snarled. As he was speaking, he started to rise and the other two salesmen duplicated his action. "We ain't the sort to let *anybody* slicker us!"

With his face registering what seemed to be alarm, Front de Boeuf gripped the edge of the table as if to assist him and rose even faster than any of the trio. Such was the speed he employed, his chair skidded away behind him and he tipped the table over with a force that had a devastating effect upon the others around it.

Caught unawares by the rapidity with which the hitherto almost somnolent young man was moving, none of the trio had done more than raise his rump from his chair when the overturning took place. Trying to avoid being trapped, or further incommoded, Un-Mench only succeeded in tipping his seat backward and he was precipitated to the floor. Being at the opposite side to Front de Boeuf, Sheets was struck by the descending edge of the table. His chair collapsed beneath him and he too alighted supine upon the hard wooden boards. Displaying somewhat greater speed than the other two, Dishpan contrived to extricate himself by driving his chair backward. Although he staggered a few paces on reaching his feet, he remained upon them.

"Good heavens, how *clumsy* of me!" the massive young man gasped in a tone redolent of contrition. "Are you all right, Sheets?"

While speaking the second sentence, Front de Boeuf started to advance as if desirous of rendering assistance to the man he named. If that was his intention, it proved less than helpful to another of the party. Because of his apparent haste and flustered condition, he stepped upon Un-Mench in passing. Being addicted to the "pleasures of the table" and having eaten an enormous breakfast that morning, in addition to an even larger meal the previous evening, the underwear salesman was unable to withstand the effect of having a boot impelled by a weight in excess of two hundred and fifty pounds descend upon his stomach. A strangled gurgle burst from him and, although the boot was removed quite soon after its arrival, he was incapable of doing anything except twitch spasmodically and gasp for breath.

Seemingly oblivious of what he had done to Un-Mench, Front de Boeuf went to where Sheets was sprawled. Bending, the massive young man took hold of the lapels of the bed linen salesman's jacket and started to haul him upward as if he weighed no more than a newborn baby. However, laudable though the action might otherwise have been, it was not brought to fruition. Having halted, Dishpan let out a bellow of rage and charged forward with his right hand going under his jacket to emerge gripping a wicked-looking blackjack. Apparently the sound startled the massive young man, with an adverse effect upon Sheets. The grasp on his jacket was released in a way that gave him a shove and, once more, he was propelled to the floor. This time, the back of his head smacked down on the planks and he lost all interest in everything for some time.

Turning with a clumsy pivoting motion, Front de Boeuf flailed wildly with his arms as if trying to maintain his balance. This proved most unfortunate for Dishpan. Advancing recklessly, he was caught with the back of the massive young man's right hand. It arrived with a force that, in addition to causing him to lose his grip on the blackjack, sent him in a reeling twirl far in excess of the haste caused by his hurried departure from the table. Halted by collid-

ing against the wall, he rebounded and went down in no
better condition to continue the intended attack than either of his companions.

"All right!" growled a surly voice. "What the hell's coming off here?"

"Just an *accident*," Trilby replied, turning a less than
friendly gaze toward the speaker whom he had seen standing and watching from just outside the front entrance until
after the trouble ended. "Ain't *nothing* for you to worry
on."

Lumbering through the batwing doors while he was
speaking, Jack Tinker kept his gaze on Front de Boeuf and
ignored the bartender. About six feet tall, he had sullen
porcine features and was heavily built, but clearly out of
condition. He wore a cheap three-piece brown suit, a
grubby white shirt without a collar, and a Stetson. The
shotgun in his right hand served to augment the Colt
Peacemaker in a cross-draw holster on his waistbelt.
Pinned to his food-stained vest, the tarnished badge he was
deliberately bringing into view by pushing open his jacket
with his left thumb was that of a deputy town marshal. He
claimed to be the senior of the four who served in that
capacity; therefore, he was in command when the marshal
was absent for any reason. However, it was no secret
around Abilene that his sole qualification for the post was
being the mayor's brother-in-law.

"What started the fuss?" Tinker growled, studying the
massive young man's returned appearance of mild-man-
nered sloth to make sure he could exert his authority without danger to himself.

"These gentlemen grew angry because I won at cards,"
Front de Boeuf replied. "In fact, they even implied I was
cheating."

"Were they right?" Tinker asked, and decided belatedly
that such a question could provoke a hostile response, so

he transferred his left hand to the foregrip of the shotgun to heft it in what he considered to be a threatening fashion.

"Good heavens, *no*," Front de Boeuf answered, sounding horrified and almost on the point of bursting into tears. "Ask the gentleman behind the bar. He's been watching us on and off all the time we were playing."

"I never *saw* the young feller do anything wrong," Trilby asserted truthfully, striding around the bar. "Way he played, he's no Joe Brambile nor Pappy Maverick and he for sure ain't no Last-Card Johnny Bryan neither."

"Sounds like he wasn't cheating, then," Tinker mumbled reluctantly, knowing the first two men named had the reputation for being completely honest—albeit very efficient —professional gamblers. However, the third came into a vastly different category and had acquired his nickname due to the notoriously potent improvement his hands all too frequently received from the last card he gave himself when dealing in a game of stud poker. "But that warn't no call for him to start beating up on 'em."

"I didn't see no 'beating up' neither," Trilby corrected, despite having suspicions that there was far more to the massive and apparently lethargic young man than met the eye. He also considered the trio had not only received no more than they deserved for their attempts at cheating, but might have counted themselves fortunate that nothing worse happened. "They fell down trying to get clear when the table was tipped over accidental like, and he was trying to help 'em up again when things sort of went wrong."

Hearing the derisive chuckles and sardonic laughter that arose all around the room, a scowl creased Tinker's far from handsome face. Knowing he was not as liked and respected as was his superior in the Town Marshal's office, the feeling that the customers were enjoying themselves at his expense rankled. He also realized there was nothing he could do to avenge himself upon them. However, he decided he must make some gesture to try to reassert his authority before leaving, and he considered the big young dude offered the best opportunity for bringing this about.

"All right, feller," the peace officer said, endeavoring to sound as authoritative as he believed Marshal Markham would in similar circumstances. "Looks like you're in the right of it *this* time, but I don't want to see you in no more trouble or fuss while you're around my town."

"Don't worry, sir," Front de Boeuf answered mildly and, apparently, with respect tinged by awe. "I'll do my best to see you don't catch me doing *anything* wrong."

"Good evening, Mr. Merridew," Cuthbert Alan Bleasdale the Third greeted. Striding swiftly across the dining room of the Railroad Hotel, he spoke with the kind of tone he reserved for when addressing somebody who he believed might be of use to him. "I thought I'd be seeing you at the livery barn this afternoon."

"Nope," the horse buyer for the United States Army replied with no great display of cordiality, deciding the other man had come to seek an invitation to join him for a meal at his expense. "Seeing's how you don't have anything to offer me, I figured I'd leave it until Monday."

"How do you know I don't have anything?" Bleasdale asked, despite the report he had received from Dick Lester regarding the activities of Jessica Front de Bouef giving him an idea of what had happened. "There're plenty of horses in the corrals."

"And I've had a long talk with the lady who owns them."

"Just a talk?"

"Nope. She sold 'em all to me."

"She's a personal friend of mine, so I hope you gave her a good price."

"Good enough," Merridew answered. Despite the claim to friendship, he considered it was highly unlikely the owner of the livery barn would accept the kind of favors he was anticipating for lowering the cost of the herd when making the deal with Jessica. "For what they are."

"There's nothing wrong with them," Bleasdale lied, such being an almost instinctive reaction when the excessive price and poor quality of horses he was selling came under discussion. Wondering whether he might have made an error, despite feeling certain the horse buyer would not have given anywhere near the actual figure for such a sorry collection of animals, he elected to be frank about the deal he had made. "I'd say she got a *bargain* for two thousand five hundred dollars."

"Two thousand five hundred?" Merridew repeated in tones of disbelief.

"That's what she paid me," Bleasdale confirmed, taking out the bank draft and extending it so the amount written upon it could be read. Wondering if he might get a hold over the other man should a larger sum of Government money have been paid so as to obtain favors of a sexual nature from the well-endowed and undeniably beautiful Southron woman, he went on, "How much did she stick you for?"

"Well now, I wouldn't exactly call it being *stuck*," Merridew replied, guessing what prompted the view of the sum of money he had been given. Then a sensation of malicious pleasure came to him as he remembered what Jessica had told him of her plans and he drew a certain conclusion for the reason behind her intention to depart the following morning. "I only handed over *one* thousand and they're mine now. Which I've got a bill of sale to *prove* it."

"Only a *thousand*?" Bleasdale gasped, ignoring for the moment the implication of an indisputable change of ownership.

"That's all," Merridew confirmed.

"Goddamn it!" Bleasdale spat out, and his eyes went to

the bank draft. "Why'd she buy 'em off me for two thousand five hundred and let you have 'em for only a thousand?"

"She allowed it was for a quick cash sale."

"A *cash* sale?"

"Why sure. She reckoned's how she needed the cash because she's leaving town come tomorrow morning."

"Is she, by God?"

"Sure," Merridew affirmed, then decided to get one point settled pertaining to his original suspicions over the reason for the visit by the local horse trader. "She's coming to have dinner with me in a few minutes, so I won't be able to ask you to join me."

"I *understand*," Bleasdale declared in a tone implying he knew there was more than just a harmless and innocent dinner in the horse buyer's mind when delivering the invitation to the woman. However, to do him justice, he had not come with the hope of obtaining an excellent free meal on this occasion. He had heard from Lester, who had been close enough to see what was taking place although unable to hear anything being said, that money had changed hands before they parted company. It was this, not hoped-for hospitality, that had prompted him to pay the call. Although a surge of anger filled him as he thrust the bank draft back into his pocket, he managed to keep it from showing. He was helped in this by the thought of how he could take revenge upon Merridew while carrying out the more important task of ensuring his financial interests were protected. "And I'll be going. I only dropped by to ask whether you'd want any horses. There're a bunch out at my ranch that I reckon you'll be willing to take."

"I'll look them over on Monday," Merridew promised, somewhat surprised that the other was taking the discovery so calmly. However, his attention was distracted by the sight of his guest entering the lobby. It was obvious she had taken care to dress in an especially attractive fashion for the occasion. In addition to being exquisitely bejeweled, the simple black satin evening gown she wore clung snugly to her "hourglass" lines and emphasized them even more than had the attire she was wearing at their last meeting. "And I'll see you then."

"That suits me fine," Bleasdale answered, and swung around to hurry away.

"I see you've had a visitor," Jessica remarked, as the horse buyer strode from the dining room to pass her.

"Yes," Merridew admitted, running a lascivious eye over the woman's curvaceous figure—which his horse buyer's instincts assessed was far from being produced by artificial aids alone—and savoring in anticipation the pleasures he felt sure would be forthcoming after the meal. "He was trying to sell me some horses he's got out at his ranch, but I told him I won't be talking business before Monday. Shall we go in and have dinner?"

"Certainly," Jessica assented, and allowed her host to take her by the arm while leading her to a secluded table at the side of the room.

From then on, everything appeared to be going as Merridew wanted. As he was sure would be the case, the food was excellent and, despite claiming she should not as it had the effect of lowering her inhibitions, Jessica willingly shared the bottle of champagne that followed it. Furthermore, when he hinted that she might like to have some more of the liquor in his room to toast the deal they had concluded, she showed no hesitation before agreeing.

"Here she is, Deputy Tinker!" Bleasdale announced in a carrying voice, coming into the dining room followed by the peace officer to confront the couple as they were crossing toward the door. He was delighted to see that everybody else present stopped whatever they were doing and looked his way. "Arrest her for trying to swindle me with a fake bank draft!"

"Sure thing," Tinker assented, feeling just as pleased at finding himself at the center of attention in such luxurious surroundings. "I figured there was something wrong with her when I saw her son'd rooked and abused three fellers he'd suckered into playing cards with him. This'll teach 'em they can't play them kind of games in *my* bailiwick."

"Just take a look at what we've got here, gals!" suggested the biggest of the three garishly dressed women Deputy Marshal Jack Tinker had brought into that portion of the town's jail reserved for female prisoners. Although the other cell was empty, the new arrivals had been placed in the one that was already occupied. "They've sure got them a high-toned lobby-lizzy visiting tonight."

Seated on the lower of one set of double bunks, Jessica Front de Boeuf did not appear to be giving the speaker any more attention than she had since the trio arrived.

Despite Titus Merridew having tried to persuade the peace officer it was not necessary, acting as had been suggested by Cuthbert Alan Bleasdale the Third when lodging the complaint—although ordered might have been a more accurate term—he had insisted upon handcuffing Jessica before escorting her along the busy street from the Railroad Hotel to the Town Marshal's office. There, he had had the wife of another deputy employed for such duties subject her to the kind of search and treatment given to the usual variety of female prisoners. She did not have any of the money received earlier from the horse buyer on her person, but was made to remove all her jewelry and place it in an envelope, which, as a precaution against later claims that some was missing, she and the woman had marked with their signatures over its sealed-down flap. With this formality completed, although he would usually have left the incarceration to Mrs. Hogan, he had placed her in a cell and went off to carry out the rest of the horse trader's instructions.

Calling at the respectable rooming house where Jessica and her son were staying, wanting to boost his prestige among such potentially influential people, Tinker had not troubled to keep the reason for his visit from being overheard by the other occupants. Much to his annoyance, one of them had been a prominent lawyer visiting from Topeka and had immediately offered to act on behalf of the Front de Boeufs. While Counselor Arnold J. Grosvenor had admitted that the serious nature of the charge against Jessica precluded any chance of her being released on bail, he had been equally adamant that there was no legal reason why her son should be taken into custody when the peace officer had suggested doing so. However, he had offered to hold the one thousand dollars received from the U.S. Army's horse buyer as surety that the young man would remain in town until the matter could be brought before the judge on Monday.

Although Tinker could not be rated among the most intelligent men in Abilene, thinking about the reputation of the legal adviser for his prisoner, he was more than a little perturbed as he had set off to do the second part of Bleasdale's bidding. However, he was also aware that he was in no position to avoid obeying his instructions. Nevertheless, he decided to take precautions. Instead of going to see Big Kate Carteret personally at her place of business, he had had the proposition suggested by the horse trader put to her by an acquaintance whose known—albeit unreported—dishonest activities made it impossible for him to refuse to help. Big Kate, having found business slack and needing the money, accepted the offer.

In accordance with the plan, the prostitute and two of her companions were "arrested" by Tinker for "disturbing

the peace." Accompanied by Anna Longton and Jane
Drabble, whose presence was mainly to serve as witnesses
testifying to her "veracity" when she had later to explain
what caused the trouble she was hired to make, she was
taken and placed in the cell with the intended victim. Before doing this, however, they too had been searched by
the female deputy and had been compelled to shed their
rings and other jewelry. Even if this had not been standard
procedure, bearing in mind what he was told by Bleasdale,
the peace officer would have insisted upon it being done to
ensure no seriously disfiguring injuries were inflicted that
might influence a jury to sympathy when the trial of Jessica
Front de Boeuf took place.

"Hey, *you*!" Kate snapped in an even louder voice, stepping in front of the black-haired woman when there was no
response to her comment. Standing on widespread legs
and with arms akimbo, her sturdy body was set off by a
gaudy dress of flimsy material that clung so tightly it suggested there was only the minimum of undergarments beneath it. "I want that bunk!"

"Are you speaking to *me*?" Jessica inquired, looking up
as if noticing she was no longer alone for the first time.

"Who the hell else?" the big prostitute demanded, exuding menace and confident that size, weight, strength, and
experience were all in her favor.

"Then I would much rather you kept your remarks to
yourself," Jessica stated. "And I'm *not* going to move!

"You aren't, huh?" Kate spat out, and prepared to
launch the attack she had been paid to carry out.

Studying their intended victim on their arrival, the trio
considered there would be no difficulty in earning the
money they had been offered. Not one of them had attached any significance to the way in which the Southron
woman was seated. Leaning back a little, supported by her
hands on the bunk behind her, she had her left leg raised

so its foot rested upon her right knee. The posture was not graceful, nor did it seem to be in any way dangerous. However, looks proved very deceptive.

When Trudeau Front de Boeuf had been threatened with assault by the three salesmen at the Scranton Saloon, everything that followed had had the appearance of taking place by accident. The same did not apply where his mother was concerned. For all the impression she gave of being a wealthy and pampered Southron, presumably one from a sheltered background that left her so naive she allowed herself to be tricked into paying a far larger sum for the bunch of poor-quality horses than they were worth, her response to the threat was more suited to a female roughhouse brawler well versed in such matters. In fact, despite having a well-deserved reputation for toughness, the biggest of the prostitutes would have been hard-pressed to achieve better results.

Showing a remarkably swift grasp of the situation, Jessica took very effective means to counter it. Before Kate could deliver the intended assault, the raised leg was swiftly thrust forward. Emerging from under the skirt that had kept it concealed until that moment, the foot proved to be in a sturdy riding boot and not something more delicately feminine. What was more, the kick was sent with considerable power and precision to the point where it would do most good—or harm—dependent upon one's point of view.

Caught at the junction of her spread-apart thighs by the hard heel of the boot, if she had remained capable of conscious thought, Kate might have regretted the weather being so clement that she was wearing only the minimum of clothing over the point of impact. As it was, a strangled screech burst from her. Under her heavy makeup, her face turned an ashy grayish-green and, with hands flying to the stricken region, she began to hunch her body forward. Unfortunately for her, she was not permitted to gain even what little relief her actions might have given. Bringing down the foot and thrusting herself from the bunk, Jessica caught the big prostitute's throat with her left hand. The fingers and thumb were buried on either side of the wind-pipe, and to the accompaniment of further sounds of stran-gulation, Kate was pushed erect again.

"Hey!" Anna yelped, staring in amazement and then starting to move forward with the intention of helping her friend.

Before the second prostitute could come within range, Jessica gave a thrust that sent Kate stumbling backward to crash in a seated position against the wall. In a continua-tion of the move, the black-haired Southron whipped around a backhand slap that proved as potent as the one delivered apparently by accident when her son had been attacked earlier in the day. Caught by the blow, Anna was knocked in just as helpless a twirl against the opposite wall from where she bounced to fall dazed and bewildered onto her stricken companion.

Nor did Jane prove any more successful. Like Anna, she had expected to be no more than a witness to the beating up of the other prisoner and to support the story told about it. However, she too was aware that some form of more positive action would now be expected from her. What was more, she was just as sure the reaction to hear-ing she had refrained from helping would be painful in the extreme if the larger of her companions learned this was the case. With that in mind, letting out a howl that was as much fear as anger, she lunged out of the corner into which she had retreated involuntarily, and her fingers reached for hair. She did not achieve her purpose. Before they could arrive at their objective, two hands passed be-tween her arms and knocked them apart. Then, allowing her no opportunity to respond to the changed situation, a set of hard knuckles caught the side of her jaw and she was sent back in the direction from which she had come to alight with a bone-numbing jolt on her rump.

"What the hell's going o—!" demanded the female deputy, having heard the commotion and come to investigate. Knowing the reputation of the largest prostitute, the sight that met her gaze brought her words to a halt. Lowering the bucket of cold water that she had brought to use in quelling the disturbance, she went on in tones of bewilderment, "Did *you*—"

"Do I look like the kind of a person who would behave in such a fashion?" Jessica queried, and judging from her demeanor, butter would have been hard-pressed to melt in her mouth. "They began to quarrel amongst themselves and, after one was knocked down, the other two fell against the wall and stunned one another."

"They did, huh?" the woman deputy said, eyeing the black-haired Southron in a speculative fashion.

No fool, in fact Marshal Markham frequently claimed that—despite having no official status and only being paid for the duties she performed because he had insisted upon it—she was the best and most intelligent assistant he possessed, Mrs. Hilda Hogan found much about the situation puzzling. She had been surprised when Tinker insisted on taking first the Southron woman and then the three prostitutes into the female section of the jailhouse. Usually, he avoided doing any more work than he was compelled to do and left such tasks to her. More in keeping with his character, he had left, supposedly to make his rounds of the town, on emerging from locking up his latest prisoners and had not returned.

Knowing Big Kate's reputation as a trouble-causer and having no reason to disbelieve Tinker's claim that the trio were brought in for disturbing the peace, Mrs. Hogan had not been surprised when she heard the commotion from the cell. Therefore, she had arrived on the scene expecting to have to stop a fight between them. Before she could do more than start thinking of how ill-advised Tinker had been when incarcerating them with the other woman, the ramifications of the sight that greeted her drove everything else from her head. Nor, in her opinion, did the explanation she had received do anything to clarify the situation.

"They *did*," Jessica confirmed. "And I would like to protest about them having been put in this cell with me."

"Yeah," the deputy answered, deciding to let her suspicions go unchecked and taking the ring of keys from her waistbelt. "Jack Tinker shouldn't've done that. Come on, I'll put you in next door."

"That's most considerate of you," Jessica declared. "And I won't forget it when I've got this whole unfortunate business cleared up on Monday morning."

"And, purely as a result of *unsupported* suppositions, my client suffered the humiliation of being arrested and marched in handcuffs through the street in public view without even having been questioned and granted an opportunity to refute the allegations made against her," Counselor Arnold J. Grosvenor boomed in his most imposing courtroom tones, glaring around him in the manner that had impressed judges and, more usefully where the needs of his clients were concerned, juries whenever he appeared as defense attorney. Although neither were present on this occasion, he considered his behavior justified and continued, "Then, as if that was not injustice enough, she was held prisoner in the company of women of ill repute until this morning!"

"She got treated real good all the time she was there," Deputy Marshal Jack Tinker claimed from where he was standing in a sullen slouch at the rear of the room.

Before he completed the attempt at exculpation, the

surly-looking peace officer began to wish he had not drawn attention to himself. He had already been subjected to a less than pleasant interview with his superior and was left in no doubt that he was considered to have acted in a most ill-advised fashion.

It was shortly after nine o'clock on Monday morning and the office of the Town Marshal was more crowded than it usually was at that hour of the first day of the week.

Being aware of the kind of a First Deputy he had had foisted upon him by Mayor David Shipman, Town Marshal Stanley Woodrow Markham had been surprised to receive a visit from Tinker while he was having breakfast at his home. At first, unaware that his presence so early in the day was in itself a source of suspicion due to his lazy habits, the bulky and surly peace officer had tried to give the impression that he believed he had upheld the law in a satisfactory fashion while his superior was absent. Nevertheless, it was obvious that he was far from happy with the results of his efforts. Nor had Markham considered his poorly concealed perturbation unjustified as he described how he had decided the complaint lodged by Bleasdale required that he should arrest Jessica Front de Boeuf.

Subjecting Tinker to a far from amicable interrogation while hurrying to his office, every instinct the Marshal possessed—being a lawman of long experience—warned him things might not be quite so straightforward as they appeared on the surface. Learning of the incident in the cell from Mrs. Hilda Hogan, who had remained on duty all night, he had heard nothing to make him change his mind. When asked what had caused the trouble, the three prostitutes had substantiated the story told by the other prisoner when explaining how they were found in the position that so puzzled his female deputy. Nevertheless, after having seen and spoken with Jessica, he had suspected there was more to the incident than that. The discovery that she had obtained the legal services of Counselor Grosvenor, whose reputation was well known to—if not respected by—peace officers throughout Kansas, struck him as offering further proof of his supposition.

Being aware of just how serious the situation could be, Markham decided to take every possible precaution. To achieve this, he had assembled all the parties who, he believed, would be most interested in the outcome of the affair. Gathered from their homes by Mrs. Hogan and the First Deputy were the Mayor, Bleasdale, and—at Tinker's suggestion—his brother-in-law, Counselor Richard P. Maher. Knowing his evidence would be crucial, the Marshal had also sent for Gaylord Benskin, the president of the Cattleman's Bank, and wishing to learn all the facts, arranged for Titus Merridew to attend. To protect himself against later claims that her side of the affair was not heard, he had insisted that Jessica was present and, although stressing that he was only holding an informal hearing to ascertain the facts, he acceded to her request that her son, Trudeau, should bring their attorney.

When asked to tell his side of the matter, although Maher was clearly impressed and not a little perturbed on learning the identity of the other lawyer, Bleasdale was confident that the outcome of the "informal hearing" was a foregone conclusion. Before his brother-in-law could intervene, darting a malignant glare at Jessica—who had obviously escaped the additional punishment he had hoped to have had inflicted and, despite the attempt having failed, for which he had already paid—he had explained that he was to have been the victim of a confidence trick. Much to his annoyance, instead of immediately accepting his version, the Marshal had not objected when Grosvenor began to speak in her defense.

"The treatment my client was accorded while in custody is neither here nor there," Grosvenor stated, eyeing Tinker with disdain. "What is of the *greatest* importance is that she should *never* have been subjected to any of it."

"Like he—" Bleasdale began, but a kick on the ankle from his brother-in-law brought the words to a halt.

"Come now, Counselor," Maher said, after directing a furiously prohibitive glare at the horse trader. "This woman—"

"I prefer my client to be addressed as 'Mrs. Front de Boeuf,' Counselor," Grosvenor put in.

"Very well," Maher assented, realizing he was up against a master of every aspect of their profession and feeling very much a novice in comparison. "*Mrs. Front de Boeuf* gave my client a bank draft for a considerable sum of money to purchase a herd of horses and, within a *remarkably* short time, sold them at a considerable loss for *cash.*"

"And what makes that an illegal transaction calling for her to be arrested and subjected to such humiliation?" Grosvenor inquired.

"She told my client she would be taking the horses away on Monday afternoon," Maher replied. "And yet he was informed by Merri—" He amended his speech as he received a cold glare from the horse buyer for the United States Army. "*Mr.* Merridew that she was planning to leave town on Sunday morning."

"Did you tell Mr. Merridew that, ma'am?" Markham queried.

"Well, yes I did," Jessica admitted. "You see, I needed cash to settle a few accounts I had acquired around town."

"But why'd you say you were leaving town the next morning?" the marshal asked.

"I'm a widow, sir," Jessica explained. "And not unattractive, if I can say it without being thought immodest. So I have had unpleasant experiences through being subjected to the unwanted attentions of gentlemen when compelled by circumstances to ask a favor." She paused and directed a smile and nod at the horse buyer before continuing, "Although, on this occasion, I found I had nothing to fear on that account. Everything about Mr. Merridew's behavior was perfectly proper. In fact, I was just about to explain I would not be leaving until Monday when I was confronted and not only arrested, but subjected to being handcuffed like a common criminal and—"

"Why'd you sell those horses for only a thousand dollars when you paid me twenty-five hundred for them?" Bleasdale demanded, displeased and alarmed by the effect upon some of the audience—including Mayor Shipman, whom he had counted upon being a supporter—when the woman's words died away as if she was too overcome by the horror of the situation to go on.

"Because, *sir,*" Jessica answered, stiffening her shoulders in a manner that implied she was struggling to regain her composure. "I had received word from a friend in Topeka that the people who were my partners had decided to back out of the deal. That meant the horses would be of no further use to me. So I decided that, even if I was unable to obtain the full amount, I would try to get back my own money which I had invested in the venture."

"Why did you go to Merridew?" Maher inquired, wishing his brother-in-law would keep quiet and leave him to handle the interrogation.

"I had heard of his integrity and the high prices he paid," Jessica explained. "So I thought I would obtain a good offer from him for the herd."

"And you asked him for *cash,*" Bleasdale pointed out, having moved beyond the reach of his brother-in-law's leg.

"I did," Jessica admitted.

"But you'd paid *me* by a bank draft!" the horse trader reminded, with the air of one who had made the most significant point of the exchange.

"Why wouldn't I pay you that way?" Jessica challenged.

"I'm hardly likely to carry twenty-five hundred dollars in my reticule, and as I explained to Mr. Merridew, there were some accounts I have with local businesspeople that I wished to settle."

"Then why didn't you settle *them* with bank drafts?" Bleasdale demanded, paying no attention to the shrug of resignation given by Maher. "Or go and get some cash from the bank to do it?"

"The bank was *closed*," Jessica pointed out. "And as I have never cared to have accounts outstanding over the weekend, considering this unfair to the people concerned, I wanted to settle them instead of waiting until Monday."

"Then you're telling us this bank draft you gave me will be made good?" the horse trader asked in a disbelieving tone, producing and tearing apart the sheet of paper. "That's what I thin—"

"Why'd you do *that*?" Benskin inquired quietly. "You could have cashed it in any time you wanted to come in this morning."

"What?" Bleasdale croaked, staring at the bank president in alarm and consternation.

"Mrs. Front de Boeuf deposited five thousand dollars with us on her arrival," Benskin elaborated, and there was a twinkle in his eyes. "So that bank draft she gave you was and *still is* perfectly good."

"G-g-g-g-*good*?" the horse trader gobbled.

"Good," Benskin confirmed.

"Are you sure the money she gave you is all right?" Bleasdale demanded, and in his perturbation, he was oblivious of the alarmed intake of breath his words elicited from Maher. "It wasn't counter—!"

"If I were you, Counselor, I would advise your client to curb his tongue," Grosvenor boomed. "He is already *deeply* involved in making slanderous accusations against my client without adding to them."

"For God's sake, Cuth!" Maher croaked in a strangled tone. "Keep quiet and leave *me* do the talking!"

"You have received most sound advice, *sir*," the Topeka lawyer declared ominously. "I don't think you realize just how seriously your unjustified accusations will be taken if they are brought before a court of law."

"Is it necessary for the matter to go that far?" Maher inquired in a sour yet hopeful voice, having noticed how the word "if" had been employed instead of "when", and realizing what this portended.

"I would say that all depends how much your client is willing to pay in recompense for the humiliation he caused Mrs. Front de Boeuf to suffer," Grosvenor replied. "And I will go further in stating we consider the sum must be adequate enough to cover the stigma he has placed upon her good name."

"That wasn't a bad weekend's work, Momma," Trudeau Front de Boeuf remarked, as he and his mother walked toward Bleasdale's livery barn on Monday afternoon. "And we didn't even have to mention Cousin Mark, Cousin Solly, or Uncle Winston, to prove we had some mighty influential kin who'd back us up."

"I'm pleased we didn't," Jessica replied. "Marshal Markham's no fool, and the last thing I'd want is for him to get in touch with any of them, especially Solomon Cole. Winston, and dear Mark in particular, would have been *tactful* for the sake of the family, but I'm afraid Solomon would feel bound by his oath of office as a U.S. Deputy Marshal and would have told the truth."

There was good reason for the massive young man to be so jubilant.

However, Jessica's sentiments were not without justification.

In fact, if Town Marshal Stanley Woodrow Markham

had overheard the conversation, it would have confirmed the suspicions he was harboring with regard to the Front de Boeufs at the conclusion of the informal hearing he had held.

While they were discussing the matter privately in another room at the jailhouse, warned by his brother-in-law that he was faced with the prospect of a costly lawsuit that he was certain to lose, Cuthbert Alan Bleasdale the Third was advised to settle the matter out of court and on the spot. Further pressure to follow this course had been provided by Mayor David Shipman on joining them. It was prompted by his realization that the town could be faced with a similarly costly suit for false arrest and, at the next election, the voters would not forget his brother-in-law was its instigator. He had been informed by Jessica this was not contemplated, as Deputy Jack Tinker had only done what he regarded as his duty, so he had considered it politic to lend support to the claim against the horse trader. After only a token resistance, albeit with bad grace, Bleasdale agreed to pay recompense of ten thousand dollars to his "victim." What was more, as "boot" for the deal, he had been required to supply her and her son with a buggy and team to take them to their next destination.

Regardless of the way they had behaved since arriving in Abilene, Jessica and her son were far from being the harmless innocents selected as potential victims by the men who fell into the traps they laid. They had numerous kinfolk who were pillars of society and respected for honesty in all matters, including the three they had mentioned. Winston Front de Boeuf was one of the pioneers of cattle raising on a large scale north of the intercontinental railroad. Youngest son of a wealthy rancher from the Big Bend country in Texas, as well as being acclaimed for other abilities, Mark Counter had acquired a well-deserved reputation as a most competent peace officer in a trail-end town. Since being appointed a United States Deputy Marshal in Kansas, Solomon Wisdom "Solly" Cole had become known for honesty and integrity.

Neither Jessica nor Trudeau Front de Boeuf could claim to possess such high moral standards. They were, in fact, the "black sheep" of their family and spent their lives involving themselves in illicit activities of various kinds. Their way of life required that they kept moving and they had come to Kansas in search of fresh victims. Nor was their presence in Abilene the result of pure chance. In accordance with their policy, they had had a most efficient associate scouting the railroad towns for a likely prospect upon whom to work a confidence trick thought up by Jessica.

Produced by a man who knew what to look for, the very thorough report from their associate suggested the Front de Boeufs had found the "mark" they wanted. It covered Bleasdale's less than savory reputation and nature, the well-filled state of his corrals, and the type of animals they held, Gaylord Benskin's habit of closing the Cattlemen's Bank early on Saturday when going for a weekend hunting trip with the town marshal, the kind of peace officers who would be available in Markham's absence, and how Titus Merridew would be in town buying horses for the United States Army. Taking all these factors into account, she had concluded Bleasdale qualified as a suitable victim and the scheme was put into operation.

Everything had gone according to plan. Nor had Trudeau Front de Boeuf's encounter with the three traveling salesmen been accidental. Having seen them operating in another town, he had selected them to bring himself to the attention of Deputy Marshal Jack Tinker in a manner calculated to arouse suspicion. While this was happening, as Jessica expected, Bleasdale had had her followed at the conclusion of the purchase of the horses. Then he and the peace officer, on learning of her negotiations with Merridew, had behaved as was anticipated. Knowing the kind of man she was up against, she had suspected the reason for the three prostitutes being put into the cell with her and had been ready to counter it. When they had recovered sufficiently to understand the situation, Jessica, wanting to avoid the way in which she had protected herself destroying her pose of well-bred innocence, had given them some of the money she had kept successfully concealed upon her person while being searched and they had agreed to "confirm" the story she had told Mrs. Hogan.

With the matter concluded in a most satisfactory fashion, the Front de Boeufs had no intention of remaining in Abilene any longer than was necessary. They had too much respect for the acumen of the Marshal to want to give him time to check up on their background. Returning to the rooming house, they had made changes to their attire to fit them for their journey and were already on their way. Having sent their belongings ahead with instructions for them to be loaded on the buggy, Jessica was dressed much as she had been when meeting Bleasdale and buying the horses. Her son had changed into a Texas-style white Stetson, a loose-fitting and open-fringed buckskin jacket over a dark-blue shirt, brown Eastern-style riding breeches, and black Wellington leg boots. However, the garments did not make him seem any more impressive or dangerous in any way.

The horses Jessica had bought and then sold to Titus Merridew were still in the corrals, but otherwise the livery barn looked deserted as she and her son arrived. Although she had expected the man who delivered their baggage to be waiting for payment, neither he nor anybody else answered her call for attention. However, when they went through the front entrance of the building, they found there were human occupants. What was more, the two men in dirty range-style clothes who confronted them obviously were not present for any harmless purpose such as helping to prepare the buggy for their use.

"Keep your mouths shut and don't make no sudden moves!" the taller of the pair growled, his voice somewhat muffled by the bandanna he had tied around his face to serve as a mask. Gesturing with the Colt Peacemaker he held, he went on, "We want *all* that money you've got and aim to have it, even if we have to *kill* you both to get it!"

Listening to Tom Clarke speaking from below his hiding place in the hayloft of the livery barn, Dick Lester, behind the bandanna he too considered was advisable to wear as a mask, grinned as he thought of the easy money they and their cousin, Michael McCann, would soon be making. It would be far in excess of anything they had previously received from Cuthbert Alan Bleasdale the Third, who had underpaid them through all the time they had been engaged in stealing and selling horses to him. Not that he suspected they had no intention of turning the money taken from the Front de Boeufs over to him and contenting themselves with the thousand dollars he had promised would be their share. Instead, as soon as it was in their possession, they would collect the horses they had waiting not too far away and head out with all speed, never to return.

To give the horse trader his due, Lester thought, everything had been as he promised when the trio had reached the barn. None of his employees were present and, on arrival, the man with the victims' baggage had proved no obstacle. Hit on the head with the barrel of Clarke's Colt, he had been rendered unconscious and unable to resist being tied up, gagged, and placed in Bleasdale's office where he would not be seen.

Climbing into the hayloft, which offered a better view of the surroundings than was obtainable at ground level, Lester had been satisfied that nobody else was in the vicinity as the couple he and his kinsmen were awaiting came into view. Studying them, despite knowing they had pulled off a mighty slick trick against Bleasdale, he had been confident they would prove easy pickings. However, instead of continuing the surveillance of the outside area as he had told the others he would do, he decided to move forward until he could watch what happened during the robbery. Having little faith in human nature as a whole and none whatsoever in his two partners possessing a sense of honesty and fair dealing, any more than he did, he wanted to make sure neither pocketed a proportion of the loot before it could be divided equally among all of them. He heard the straw-littered wooden floor creak slightly under his feet, but felt sure the sound would go unnoticed by the woman and massive young man. Nor would he have been any more concerned if he had known his movements were causing a trickle of dust and straw fragments to fall through the cracks in the boards as he approached the inner edge.

"Mercy me!" Jessica gasped, appearing to be horrified and swaying slightly. "How *frightening*. I feel I am going to have the vapors!"

"S-so do I, Momma!" Front de Boeuf seconded, looking even more terrified than his mother.

"Hey, Mick," Clarke said with a grin, glancing at the man by his side. "Did you ever see such a pa—"

Before the question could be completed, it was interrupted in no uncertain fashion.

While swaying, Jessica had started to raise her left hand. The moment it was pointing toward the speaker, who was too amused to attach any significance to the movement, flame erupted from the large brown fur muff that covered it and there was the somewhat muffled crash of a shot from a heavy-caliber revolver. Aimed in such a fashion, luck combined with the possession of considerable skill and

caused the bullet aimed by rapid instinctive alignment to
fly with unerring accuracy. A hole appeared in the center
of Clarke's forehead and the back of his skull burst open as
the lead shattered out. Spinning around, his own revolver
firing harmlessly into a bale of hay, he was going down
without knowing how the apparently foolproof plan had
gone astray.

Like his cousin, McCann had been amused at the response elicited by the threat. He had, in fact, begun to turn
his gaze in Clarke's direction with the intention of making
a similar comment. To compound his folly, on hearing the
shot, regarding Front de Boeuf as being no danger whatsoever, he swung his eyes toward the beautiful woman and
the muff from which smoke rose in a lazy curl. Not that he
was allowed more than a brief instant in which to learn
what had gone wrong.

Dismissing the young Southron as being as harmless as
he appeared proved to be a fatal mistake!

As more than one man had discovered to his cost, Trudeau Front de Boeuf, although under his domineering
mother's thumb to a certain extent, was far from being the
meek and mild milksop he frequently contrived to portray.
What was more, even without having shared her belief that
Bleasdale would try to retrieve the money taken in "recompense" by some such means, he would not have been
traveling unarmed. Concealed beneath the right side of his
jacket was a weapon of great potency, and he was as skilled
in its use as his mother was with the short-barreled Colt
Storekeeper Model Peacemaker in her muff. Knowing how
she was armed and would behave, he was ready and, taking
full advantage of the distraction she had caused, commenced his own move.

Giving a swift twist to his torso, Front de Boeuf caused
the right-side flap of his loosely hanging and unfastened
buckskin jacket to open out. Doing so exposed a Greener

converted into a "whipit" gun. In addition to other modifications, its twin barrels were reduced in length to ten inches and it was suspended by a brass eyebolt, threaded into the barrel rib, from a metal slot at the bottom of a broad leather shoulder strap. The movement of the garment allowed the gun to pivot from horizontal to vertical. Moving with a speed that was at odds with his somnolent behavior at most other times, his right hand flashed up to enfold the wrist of the stock that had been reduced until resembling the butt of an old-time flintlock pistol.

Thrusting the eyebolt free, Front de Boeuf's thumb encircled the twin hammers, and such was the strength of his massive hand, he had no difficulty in drawing them rearward. Without taking the time required to place his left hand upon the slightly shortened wooden foregrip, tilting the seven-pound—yet comparatively compact—weapon into the required point of aim, he squeezed the forward trigger. To the accompaniment of a deep coughing bellow, a red glow blossomed from the ten-gauge muzzle of the right barrel as nine .32-caliber buckshot balls were vomited forth. At such a short range, they had barely begun to spread apart when they tore into McCann's chest. Literally lifted from his feet by the sudden and violent impact, he was flung backward even more swiftly than his cousin. It was a tribute to the skill which the young Southron had acquired that, despite having to draw the far from light weapon first, its discharge took place very quickly in echo to his mother's shot.

Although startled by the way in which the situation below him had developed, Lester did not regard it as being totally out of control. He was confident that his own presence was unsuspected, and he would be able to carry out the robbery regardless of what had happened to his cousins. That he would be compelled to kill the beautiful woman and massive young man did not worry him in the

slightest. However, he was not encouraged in the decision
by the thought that he would be avenging Clarke and Mc-
Cann. Such an idea never occurred to him. They might
have been his kin, but all they now represented were two
less to share the loot and a pair of extra horses upon which
to ride relay and put added miles behind him during his
escape. Thinking of how he would spend the money taken
by the couple from Bleasdale, which would give an added
zest to his enjoyment, he started to draw his revolver and
moved forward until he was at the edge of the hayloft and
in a position to be able to use it.

Like his cousins, Lester had grossly underestimated the
potential of the pair they had considered to be defenseless
victims. Despite having been devoting most of their attention to the men confronting them, Jessica and her son had
not failed to draw the correct conclusions from hearing the
creaking of the planks and the others signs that the hayloft
had an occupant. Realizing that whoever was up there
would in all probability be an enemy, they had been compelled to deal with the more immediate problem before
satisfying themselves upon the point.

Showing no greater concern over having killed Lester
than she would when swatting a fly, Jessica turned toward
the possibility of further danger before his lifeless body
landed on the ground. Thrusting her right hand into the
muff while doing so, she closed it for added support upon
its mate. Then, thumb cocking the single-action revolver,
she brought it and its covering up to eye level and shoulder
height. Because the means of concealment she employed
prevented her from seeing the foresight on the barrel, she
was only able to aim in the approximate direction of the
masked figure that had come into view.

Swiftly though his mother moved, Front de Boeuf reacted with an even greater rapidity. Immediately upon firing his whipit gun's first load, he pivoted on his heels. Al-

though he grasped the foregrip with his left hand while doing so, he did not offer to elevate the weapon beyond waist level. Effective as its modifications made it for the purpose of concealment and combat at close quarters, they rendered sighting in the fashion of a conventional shotgun impossible. Nevertheless, even seeing the armed man appear at the edge of the hayloft—at a greater distance than his first assailant had been—did not make him consider he was ill-advised to have his weapon converted in such a fashion.

Once again the whipit gun gave its awesome boom. However, on this occasion, the buckshot balls had time to move away from one another when they arrived in the vicinity of their objective. By chance, only two of them found the intended mark and neither entered Lester's body where they would inflict a mortal wound. Not that he was left in any condition to appreciate this point. Coming closely behind the lead flying from the whipit gun, the first of three shots sent his way by Jessica missed him by a couple of inches. Although the second also went by harmlessly, it was by a lesser margin, and the next ripped into the left side of his breast to tear apart his heart. The yell of pain he let out as the buckshot punctured him was the last sound he uttered. Stumbling backward, he sprawled dying on the straw-covered floor that had betrayed him.

"No," Jessica Front de Boeuf said, shaking her head. "I've never seen any of them, to the best of my knowledge."

The sound of shooting had attracted attention and several people, including Town Marshal Stanley Woodrow Markham and, last of all on the scene, Cuthbert Alan Bleasdale the Third had come to investigate its cause. Ordering the rest of the crowd to remain outside, the peace officer had entered the livery barn with its owner on his heels. Having studied the sight, he was distracted by hearing sounds from the office that led to the discovery of the bound and gagged man. Once he was set free, and the doctor who had arrived was attending to his injured head, the peace officer had asked the question to which the black-haired Southron woman had replied.

"How about you, Mr. Bleasdale?" Markham queried, having no reason to disbelieve the statement as he knew nothing about Jessica having been followed by Dick Lester on Saturday afternoon. "I've a sort of notion I've seen them around here on occasion."

"You could have," the owner of the barn replied, contriving to appear nonchalant. "I've done business with them in the past."

"But not *recently*?" the Marshal asked.

"Not done business, as such," Bleasdale asserted, being aware that the peace officer tried to keep a watch upon all visitors to the town and wondering if the meeting he had had with Lester earlier that morning was not the secret he had assumed it to be. "But they came to see me this morning and complained my foreman wouldn't take a bunch of horses they fetched to the ranch. He told me he'd sent word there were too many vents to the brands for his liking."

"How'd they take that?" Markham inquired, having no illusions regarding the dubious ownership of some of the horses purchased by the other.

"They weren't pleased, and I got the feeling they were close to the blanket where cash was concerned," the horse trader claimed. "Hey, maybe they figured on getting back at me by robbing the barn and these tw—Mrs. Front de Boeuf and her son walked in on it, so they reckoned to rob them as well."

"Could be," the Marshal admitted. "How come none of your crew were around here?"

"I was expecting Merridew to come and collect his

horses, so I sent them to get some food before he arrived," Bleasdale answered, having anticipated the possibility of the question and provided the excuse.

"I'd like to say that I don't attach any blame *whatsoever* to Mr. Bleasdale," Jessica put in, sounding mildly magnanimous despite the conversation that was taking place having confirmed her belief that the horse trader was responsible for the attempted robbery. "As he said, they probably came to hold *him* up and decided we would do just as well as he wasn't here. It was just an accident which can happen to anybody. In fact, they do all the time."

"Thank you for saying that, Mrs. Front de Boeuf," the horse trader announced, but his gratitude was less than it might have been if he had not read the suggestion of a threat in the way the woman had looked at him while speaking. He had learned the truth about the incident at the jail, because the prostitutes had demanded extra payment for their suffering and he was compelled to agree to prevent the Marshal being informed and commencing an investigation that might lead to him. Therefore, he realized he had erred even worse than he anticipated when forming his revised judgment about the Southron woman. She was, he now believed, even more dangerous than he assumed and capable of seeking revenge in a most painful fashion. Deciding an absence from Abilene for some time would be in order, he continued, "My only regret is that you were put through such an experience."

"It was *shocking*," Jessica declared.

"You stood up to it right well, ma'am," Markham praised. "How come you and your son can handle guns well enough to do it, though?"

"I considered it advisable for Trudeau and I to learn to protect ourselves as we would be traveling among *Yankees,* sir," Jessica replied. "And I trust we will be permitted to go on our way as we planned?"

"I've got no call at all to hold you for *anything,* ma'am," Markham answered. Thinking of the suspicions he harbored about the woman and her son, he went on with a wry smile, "Fact being, although it should be the sheriff's boys's does it, I'm going to have a couple of my deputies escort you until you're out of Dickinson County. As things stand, that's the *most* I can do with you."

J.T. EDSON

Brings to Life the Fierce and Often Bloody Struggles of the Untamed West

_THE FASTEST GUN IN TEXAS	20818-3	$3.99
_ALVIN FOG, TEXAS RANGER	21034-8	$3.50
_HELL IN PALO DURO	21037-2	$3.99
_OLE DEVIL AND THE MULE TRAIN	21036-4	$4.50
_OLE DEVIL AND THE CAPLOCKS	21042-9	$4.50
_TO ARMS! TO ARMS IN DIXIE!	21043-7	$3.99
_TEXAS FURY	21044-5	$4.50
_BUFFALO ARE COMING	21046-1	$4.50
_THE SOUTH WILL RISE AGAIN	21045-3	$3.99
_MARK COUNTER'S KIN	21047-X	$4.50
_GO BACK TO HELL	21033-X	$3.50

At your local bookstore or use this handy page for ordering:

DELL READERS SERVICE, DEPT. DS
2451 South Wolf Road, Des Plaines, IL 60018

Please send me the above title(s). I am enclosing $ _____.
(Please add $2.50 per order to cover shipping and handling.) Send
check or money order—no cash or C.O.D.s please.

Dell

Ms./Mrs./Mr. _____

Address _____

City/State _____ Zip _____

DTE-12/94

Prices and availability subject to change without notice. Please allow four to six weeks for delivery.